SLOW & steady

Alphas Undone Book 2

KENDALL RYAN

Slow & Steady Copyright © 2016 Kendall Ryan

Cover design by Sara Eirew

Photography Credit: Sara Eirew

Editing by Alexandra Fresch, Angela Smith, and Ellie LoveNBooks

About the Book

When Greyson Archer tosses a twenty on the stage of a strip club, the last thing he expects to see is familiar haunted green eyes staring at him. Finley should be home raising her infant daughter and baking cookies, not tucking singles into her G-string and giving lap dances.

Greyson can't deny that he'd like his own private show, but there's not a chance in hell of that happening. The last time the former Navy SEAL saw her she was dressed in black, holding a folded flag and sobbing that it was all his fault—and he agreed with every single word. He couldn't do anything to help her then, but he can now.

Finley deserves better than this dingy club, and when an obsessed customer crosses the line, Greyson leads the rescue and will do whatever it takes to make amends for their broken past.

He never expected to want to settle down, but with Finley, everything is different. For the first time ever, he can breathe. But Greyson will have to fight for what he wants in order to keep the woman with the green eyes he's dreamed about so often.

Chapter One

Greyson

"Hi, handsome. Can I interest you in some company?" a feminine voice cooed, just barely audible over the loud thumping music.

I looked up from my glass into the heavily made-up eyes of a redhead wearing nothing but a silver G-string leaving nothing to the imagination.

A half-naked woman asking for my attention should be good thing. But she didn't stir the least bit of desire in me. "Not tonight, sweetheart, thanks."

She tipped her chin and sauntered away looking for her next conquest.

Maybe it had been a mistake coming here. None of the girls did a thing for me, and despite knocking back two whiskeys, I was still sitting there bitter and sulking.

After a horrendous day at work, rather than going home, I'd driven here – a strip club that I'd been to once or twice in the past for bachelor parties or birthdays, but that had been years ago.

Still licking my wounds over today's assignment, this had seemed like a better option than going home. The private security firm I worked for had a contract with a state prison, and today I drew the short straw – taking one of the rookies out there for a special seminar I was leading. It was supposed to be simple – instructing the guards on advanced and humane takedown strategies. But the rookie I brought with me was an ex-Marine and ended up being a hot-head with a temper. Rather than the easy day I was expecting, it turned into a damn fiasco. First he insulted the warden, then he ignored security protocols and antagonized the guards. He topped it off by almost inciting a prison riot.

And worse than all that was that it reflected on *me*. I'd had to talk my boss, and my former Navy Commander Jerry Barton, down off the ledge. He was ready to castrate us both this afternoon.

Good times.

Fucking-A.

Knocking back the remainder of my drink, I was just about to get up and leave, throw the towel in on this clusterfuck of a day, when the song changed and my eyes swung over to the stage. Amidst deep thumping beats of slow bass, wisps of smoke silhouetted a dancer in the center of the stage. I settled back in to my seat, intrigued, at least for the moment.

Starting at her feet, which were encased in a pair of sky-high red heels, my gaze wandered slowly up her body as the fog began to clear. Savoring the sight before me, I took my time, my eyes caressing shapely thighs and rounded hips with just a whisper of white lace between her legs. A flat stomach, and trim waist. My heart started to accelerate as my gaze traveled north.

Releasing the front clasp of her bra, she held the cups in place, pausing for just a fraction of a second, but enough time for me to mourn the thought of her keeping it on.

Peeling her bra slowly away, she revealed full, round breasts. A strangled groan ripped from my throat. Soft, yet perky tits, topped with rosy pink nipples that tightened in the cool air.

Jesus.

She was built just like a woman should be. Tons of soft, lightly tanned skin and ample smooth curves. My cock stood at attention, saluting her with the admiration she deserved.

She swayed, her body moving sensually, slowly, like she had all the time in the world. Unlike the other girls, she wasn't dancing *for* anyone. She was unrushed in her movements, feeling the music and rocking her hips. I imagined those hips moving over me, her soft curves in my hands, my mouth on her skin, the fingertip bruises I'd leave on those hips as I gripped her tight. My cock went as hard as steel.

Her eyes were closed and when she opened them, I about

fell out of my chair.

Deep emerald green fringed in heavy black lashes.

Fucking hell.

"Finley?" I rose out of my seat, blood pumping, and headed straight for the stage, intent on towing her little ass down from it, and shoving her in some goddamn clothes.

Her eyes found mine and widened in alarm. Then a startled little gasp pushed past her pink glossy lips.

"Sir," a booming voice asked beside me. "Are we going to have a problem?"

I stopped in my tracks, feet from the stage, fists clenched at my sides, vein no doubt popping in the side of my neck.

Realizing that if I so much as reached out my hand for her, I was going to be promptly removed from the club, and placed none-too-gingerly on my ass in the parking lot. I pulled a deep breath into my lungs. There was a no-touching rule, and I was happy to see it was being enforced. "We're good," I bit out. "A word, Finley?" My eyes stayed on hers.

Her pulse thumped in her slender neck and she gave the bouncer a tight nod. "We're okay, Bruce. Thanks." Navigating the stairs carefully, Finley came to stand before me. The music changed and another dancer took her place on stage. Even in those fuck-me pumps, she was still a good foot shorter than me.

Not to mention virtually naked. But she acted like neither of those things bothered her. Her green gaze burned fiercely, her small body tensed in a challenging posture, fearless and unashamed as a lioness. It'd been almost two years since I'd seen her, but not much had changed. Her hair was a little shorter, her eyes more guarded. And judging by the way her mouth was pulled down into a tight frown, she still hated me.

Fine by me. I deserved it.

My body was still reacting to hers and that little strip show she'd done on stage. The blood roaring through my veins, and pounding in my cock made it hard to think. The motherfucker was rock hard and ready.

Stand down, man.

"What the hell were you thinking?" she asked.

"You first, sweetheart. What the hell are you doing here?" I asked after a few tense moments.

"I'm not your sweetheart, and what does it look like?" Her narrowed eyes told me to fuck off, but she wasn't going to get rid of me that easily.

"It looked like you were shaking your ass up there for every Tom, Dick and Harry to see."

She shrugged. "I'm a stripper, Greyson, that's typically how it works."

I flattened my tongue against the roof of my mouth to temper the string of curse words I wanted to let rip. "Don't you mean *adult entertainer?*"

She rolled her eyes. "Let's not play games. Now tell me why you're here."

Wasn't it obvious? I figured she understood by now that this place was for lonely men without any real connections in their lives. I was here to forget about the miserable day I'd spent at work, and because I wasn't ready to go home alone to an empty house. "Isn't everyone here for the same thing? To drop about fifty bucks and go home with a raging boner..." I grinned at her.

"Git up there and get nekkid, doll face," a man called from the crowd.

I whipped my head around to glare at him. I was going to break that motherfucker's mouth for talking to her that way. But before I could do anything to shut him up, Finley pulled my attention back.

"I can't talk to you right now. My boss is right over there, and he expects me to be working." Her eyes flitted over to a bald man in an ill-fitting thrift store suit. His scowl etched a deep line across his forehead.

"Fine. Then I'll buy a lap dance. How much?" I pulled my wallet from my back pocket and watched as Finley's gorgeous pink lips parted in surprise.

Stand the fuck down.

"Forty, but there's no way I'm ..."

"Here's eighty. Take it." I shoved the money at her, but she took a step back.

"I'm not taking your money, Greyson."

"Well, then it looks like we're stuck, because *I'm* not leaving here without you answering a few questions. For starters, how's the baby?"

She let out a heavy sigh and shoved a hand into the mass of honey blonde curls tumbling down her shoulders. "You're incredibly annoying."

"Just a couple of minutes. You don't even have to actually do the dance." My cock begged me to reconsider, but I firmly told it to shut up. I was trying to strike a bargain here. Helping Finley was more important than feeling her delicious ass grinding into my groin...*dammit, the things I do for friendship.* "Consider the eighty bucks a fair trade for putting up with my questions."

"But my boss will—"

"Your boss can't bitch if you're getting paid. If you need an excuse, tell him I wanted to buy you a drink and complain about my day." That wasn't totally out of the ordinary—I knew at least one coworker who treated strippers like therapists. I motioned to the plush velvet lounge chairs across from us. "Come on. Those shoes have got to be killing your feet."

Her eyes cut over to the seating area with longing. "Fine. Two minutes...and I'm starting the clock now."

Once we were seated, it was nearly impossible to keep my eyes up on hers. It was like they were being pulled by a magnet down to her beautiful naked chest. Maybe forgoing the lap dance was the best move after all—I was already struggling to keep my blood in my brain, just from the sight of her. I probably couldn't string two sentences together if that incredible body was writhing against me. And something told me she knew how to move, and grind, and thrust ...

Fuck.

Finley was clearly just as uncomfortable, but in a much less enjoyable way, fidgeting on her seat and barely resisting the urge to cross her arms over her breasts. Not that she had anything to hide – she was perfection. But she'd been so bold just a few minutes ago, arguing with me by the stage. I didn't like the idea that merely being alone with me was enough to rattle her nerves. I wanted her to trust me, or at least get back on speaking terms.

She was watching me expectantly. Shit, I forgot to actually

start talking. Fucking hell. If I had any hope of surviving this conversation, she needed to cover up her chest. *Immediately.*

"Here, take my shirt," I said, unbuttoning the top few buttons on my dress shirt.

Finley rolled her eyes. "I can't wear clothes out on the floor. That's not how this works, you ass. I'm sure you're smart enough to know that much at least."

Last I knew, Finley had been widowed after I fucked up the mission Marcus and I were on – our last as Navy SEALs. She should be home raising her infant daughter and baking cookies, not tucking singles into her G-string and giving lap dances. It made me want to punch something.

Forcing oxygen into my lungs, I fought to clear my head. "Fine. Please just tell me what in the fuck you're doing working *here?*" It wasn't even a nice place. It was a fucking truck-stop strip club off the highway. Had it been a low-key gentleman's club where she served cocktails in a skimpy outfit, I might have let it slide. No, fuck that, not even then. I didn't enjoy the thought of another man's eyes on her.

Her gorgeous green eyes narrowed. "You're the last person who should be judging me."

I nodded once. "Fair enough. I've fucked up plenty, and I'm not trying to judge you, I'm just ... a little thrown off here."

She swallowed and looked down at her hands. I noticed the simple gold wedding band had been moved from her left hand to her right, like she couldn't quite part with it, but couldn't keep on like everything was normal either.

"Since …" She took a deep breath and started again. "It's just a job, I needed the money, and …" She stopped herself.

"If things were this bad, if you needed money …" Now I was the one trailing off.

Dammit. Why was one simple conversation so impossible?

"I'm doing fine. We're managing," she added.

I was pretty sure *managing* was code for *barely scraping by*. Fuck that. I'd fucked up her life once, if I could help her out now, I would. Whether she wanted that help or not. I'd like to see her try and stop me.

"That's too damn bad," I barked. "I have a responsibility to you, and Marcus wouldn't like this." My chin cut toward the action on the stage, where two girls were now performing an erotic dance together.

She closed her eyes briefly, before opening them again. Hardened green determination cut straight through me. "Marcus isn't here," she pointed out.

As if I could ever forget that fact. It still haunted me every day.

I shoved my business card at her.

"Redstone," she repeated, looking down at it.

"That has my private cell number on it."

"I don't want this. I don't want your help." She handed the card back, setting it on the small table between us.

"Please, reconsider, if things are that bad, I'll come by. Bring by groceries and dinner."

She shook her head. "It's too late for that."

"We can figure this out. I'd like to see the baby."

"I have to get back to work." Finley rose to her feet, clearly done with me and my offer for help. Groceries were a poor substitute for the husband she lost. She knew it. I knew it. And her tone left little room for argument.

Her standing here only highlighted my every mistake. It was my failure – the reason she had to resort to this. It was my responsibility to fix it. Even if she hated me ... even if she wanted nothing to do with me.

"Please." I slipped my business card under the elastic of her G-string, just above her hip, my fingers grazing the softest skin I'd ever felt. *Damn.* "Take this. Just in case."

Without a word, she turned away, marched back to the

stage, and took her spot beside another dancer, falling in to the most risqué version of line dancing I'd ever seen.

Disgusted and unable to stand by and watch her, I turned for the exit and left, my fists clenching in time with the pulsing music.

Chapter Two

Finley

Despite it being Saturday, and my day off, I was still angry over my run-in with Greyson Archer last night. *God, what an asshole.* I wasn't just mad because he'd seen me naked. I was mad because he'd seen me *vulnerable.* Barely hanging on. Hardly able to make ends meet and put food on the table for two people. Back when I was married and had Marcus, life was so different. Now I lived paycheck to paycheck in a crappy apartment and struggled to make rent. My daughter's clothes and toys were all secondhand and I hadn't had a haircut in months. There just wasn't extra money for frills.

It was bad enough that he was responsible for the mission that lost me my husband, but then he had to throw his money in my face. Offering to *help.*

Fuck that. This momma takes care of her own.

"Mommy?" Maple asked.

That was one of two words that my daughter now said, and I knew I'd never get tired of hearing it.

"Yes, baby?" I stroked her pale blonde hair back from her face as she gazed up at me with the big green eyes she'd inherited from me. "Should we make dinner?"

She nodded and toddled into the kitchen.

Peering into the fridge to look for ingredients, my thoughts began to wander.

Greyson. I hadn't seen him since the funeral, and I'd forgotten the effect he could have on me. He was six foot four inches of solid muscle with dark eyes that always looked haunted and an aura that screamed badass.

Well, he might be a former SEAL, but that didn't mean he got to march into my life and dole out orders. There had been a time when I'd thought Greyson was a stand-up guy. Marcus had obviously trusted him. But look where that trust had gotten him—a cold six feet under. And now Greyson was the kind of pathetic asshole who hung out at trashy strip joints and bothered the dancers. If he had ever been a hero, he was certainly a zero now. No matter how stunningly attractive he was, or how good he smelled.

Shaking the thoughts away, I grabbed a sticky jar of grape jelly and a loaf of bread. God, last night had been crazy. He'd seen me at my worst – and I'd just sat there and listened to him ramble on without standing up for myself.

Up on stage, I was a professional performer wearing my work *uniform*. I had nothing to be self-conscious about. But somehow, just the sight of Greyson pierced my armor. Suddenly

I was just a half-naked woman, sitting alone in a dark corner with a man...almost rubbing my ass in his lap. A shiver ran through me. I'd been relieved and oddly disappointed when he took back his request for a lap dance.

Well, none of that mattered anyway. After almost two years without a word from him, I had to believe that last night was a one-time thing. I wouldn't hear from him again.

I could see right through that offer of his. He only gave a shit about our position because he felt responsible for putting us there in the first place. Well, good—he *was* responsible. He *should* feel bad. All the more reason why I didn't need to help soothe his guilt. I stroked men's egos enough at work, and I got paid well for it. I'd be damned if I gave Greyson that service for free. I had better things to focus my emotional energy on. Whatever favors he did us, they wouldn't be worth it in the end.

Hopefully he'd gotten the picture last night. Now that he knew I wouldn't play along with his redemption kick, he was sure to get bored and give up on us. I ignored the twinge of loneliness that triggered. We didn't need him. *I* certainly didn't need him. Greyson wouldn't have stuck around anyway; once he felt like he'd done his good deed, he'd ride off into the sunset again, leaving us right back at square one. It was better to nip this in the bud before it even started.

A knock at the door snapped me out of my daydream.

Unease settled in the pit of my stomach; no one ever knocked on my door. Could it be a bill collector? Fuck, I thought I'd made all our minimum payments for this month on time. But there was always some hidden fee, some surprise deadline, some fine-print bullshit meant to nickel-and-dime us out of an honest living.

Setting the ingredients on the counter, I lifted Maple into my arms and headed for the front door.

"Yes?" I asked loudly through the thick wood. I didn't have a peephole, because my stupid landlord never got around to installing one, and I wasn't about to open the door up for just anyone.

"Finley? It's Grey," a masculine voice rumbled.

Motherfucker.

I didn't bother asking him how he found out where I lived. He worked for a private security firm. I was pretty sure he could get the records to my last Pap smear if he wanted to badly enough. The man had connections. And balls of steel, apparently, if showing up here tonight said anything.

Knowing how much Greyson could dig up on me should have been unnerving. But for whatever reason, I didn't feel like I was being stalked. Why wasn't I more scared or pissed off? Why did my gut tell me I could trust Greyson? Maybe I was just relieved that he wasn't some bill collector nagging me about late fees. This was a different kind of interruption entirely—one I could send packing if he annoyed me.

"Can I help you?" I asked through the locked door.

"Open the door," he said, his voice unamused.

With a grumbled curse under my breath, I unbolted the dead lock, and pulled it open.

"Hey." His voice was soft as he took in the view – me in an old t-shirt and yoga pants – hair up in a messy ponytail, with a baby on my hip. "Wow. She's beautiful. She looks just like you."

Surely he hadn't just called me beautiful. I straightened my shoulders, tightening my grip on Maple. I wanted to ask him what the fuck he was doing here, but I was trying to cut out cursing for my daughter's sake. "Why are you here?"

He held up a brown paper bag from the local organic grocery store – the one too expensive for me to shop at. I drove an extra ten minutes to go to the mega-mart in the next town over, where the aisles were wide and prices were rock bottom.

"I thought I made my point clear last night. Have you guys eaten?" He lowered the bags, but his eyes drilled into me. A little shiver tingled at the base of my spine.

The scent of mouth-watering food called to me. Much more than the stale bread and jelly in my kitchen did, but he would never know that. "Actually I was just about to start dinner."

"Come on, it's one meal. I even asked the lady at the deli what a toddler could eat. There's homemade mac and cheese in here."

"We don't accept charity."

"Dammit, Finley—"

"And don't curse in front of my daughter."

"Shit." He took a deep breath. "I mean, *shoot*. Let me start over."

I motioned for him to say his piece. Clearly he wasn't leaving until he got something off his chest.

"Last night was …" He paused, frowning. "It was *unexpected*. And I think there's a few more things that need to be said between us. Whether you want to do that tonight, or not, I still would like for you to enjoy this dinner."

The food smelled amazing and the idea of not having to cook and clean up on my night off sounded even better. "Fine. Thanks." I made a grab for the bag, but Greyson was faster. He held onto the bag and let himself in, essentially inviting himself over for dinner. I guess the food wasn't just for me and Maple. I should have known.

"One dinner. And this doesn't change anything," I said.

"I know that."

Seeing my place through his eyes, I was embarrassed. It never bothered me before that my furniture didn't match, or that my carpeting was worn and stained. I was doing the best I could – playing both mom and dad to my little girl.

"What's her name?" he asked, following me into the kitchen.

I set the bag of food on the kitchen table, and put Maple in her high chair. "Maple."

"Sweet," he replied.

An involuntarily and rare smile crossed my lips. "Yeah. She is." She was my saving grace.

"You sell the house?" he asked while I grabbed plates from the cupboard.

I nodded. "It was either that or be foreclosed." He was referring to the home Marcus and I had painstakingly restored one summer while he was on leave. Built last century with a huge front porch, we dreamed about filling all the bedrooms. It was our sanctuary. But after the stress of losing my husband, I went on bedrest for much of my pregnancy and couldn't work. Then Maple was born early and the extended hospital stay caused me to rack up medical bills into the tens of thousands. Even my veteran's spousal benefits could only stretch so far.

"We've lived here almost a year now," I added.

"And you've been working at the club all that time?" he asked.

"Yes." What led him in last night, I had no idea. He obviously wasn't a regular customer.

He made a grunted sound of disapproval, but didn't push it further. Which was good, because I still had half a mind to throw him out of my apartment.

I scooped some macaroni and cheese onto Maple's plastic princess plate while Greyson served us roasted chicken and rosemary potatoes.

The food looked great and smelled incredible, so at least there was that.

"I really don't like you working there," he said after several moments of silence.

"I really don't care what you like or don't like. It's not your choice where I work." I shoveled a bite of food into my mouth.

He inhaled deeply, nostrils flaring, and obviously swallowing down whatever else he was about to say.

It wasn't the worst place in the world to work. The money

was decent, and like many of the women here, where else would I go? If I had employable skills, I wouldn't be making my living grinding against a pole four nights a week.

But honestly, I liked the camaraderie. Backstage with the girls in our dressing room – it could be a hit reality show. Some of the comments and stories I overheard were hilarious. Since I was always either working or caring for Maple, the club was pretty much my only social life, and I'd developed some great unexpected friendships. But then there was the ugly stuff, too. Things I'd rather not see. Like when Bree, who said she'd been clean for three years dropped a little bag of white powder on the floor from her purse. Some of the girls working here had issues, and that was hard. But most were just regular women trying to make a living the best way they knew how. And for the most part, the customers were decent to deal with, too.

The one creepy exception to that rule was this guy named Brant. Middle-aged, balding, sad beady eyes. He'd started showing up at about the same time I began working there. Now he rarely missed a shift that I worked. It was getting ridiculous. No one should go to a strip club that often. Even if he had no life at all, there had to be better ways to spend his time. He should go learn to paint or something, for Christ's sake. Not sit in his favorite seat and stare at me, day after week after month. Not try to monopolize my lap dances or buy me cocktails as an opening for his awkward brand of flirting. He always tipped extremely well, so putting up with him was in my best interests, but his puppy-dog gaze made my skin crawl. One night, he had actually brought me a long-stemmed red rose. As if that would flatter me. Did he not realize that being nice to men—literally any man in the room—was part of my job description?

At the thought of Brant's tainted generosity, my bite of mac 'n cheese stuck in my throat. Suddenly I couldn't take the strained silence anymore. I'd had enough of men who didn't understand boundaries. Men who thought they knew what I needed better than I did. Neither Brant nor Grey cared about my actual opinions. I wasn't a real person to them, only a stage prop. They just wanted to live out their own fantasies of saving the damsel in distress: *Poor single mom. Poor stripper. Oh, you poor, poor thing.*

Some tiny part of me knew I was blowing this way out of proportion, but that whisper of calm rationality came too late. Fueled by wounded pride, my anger churned harder and harder like a runaway train, too fast for my better judgment to catch up. Why had I acted even the least bit polite, accepting Greyson's intrusive questions and condescending gestures? I needed to know what this charade was all about. Right fucking now. And if I didn't like what I heard, I'd put my foot down, no matter how delicious this dinner was.

I watched his face carefully as I asked, "Why are you here, Greyson? Trying to play knight in shining armor?"

His fork paused halfway to his mouth. He sighed through

his nose, lips pressed in a tight line, then replied evenly, "No, Finley. I'm trying to help. That's it."

My heart pounded even faster. But as hard as I searched his dark eyes, I found no trace of dishonesty. He truly didn't want anything other than to give us what we needed—what we really needed, not just what felt good to give. He wasn't a false savior who would swoop in later and demand a return on his investment. And even if he did want that self-congratulatory high of being a good Samaritan...as long as he kept it to himself and didn't expect me to fawn over him, then maybe that wasn't so bad.

Wait, what was I thinking? This wasn't just any man sitting in front of me. No matter his good intentions, he couldn't bring Marcus back from the dead.

Maple's squeals of delight interrupted my sour thoughts. I added a little more food to her plate.

Blinking back to reality, I noticed that Greyson still hadn't moved his fork. He was waiting to hear my response.

With no real clue what to say, I just huffed, "Good. Because I stopped believing in fairy tales a long time ago."

Silence descended as we resumed eating. All I could think about when I looked at him, no matter how kind he seemed or how striking he looked, was that he was the reason I lost my husband. That wasn't something I'd ever get over. *Ever.*

Chapter Three

Greyson

Forcing a bite of food into my mouth, I couldn't get over how much her daughter looked like her. From her green eyes to her honey-colored hair to her delicate features. She was a miniature version of Finley and I was enthralled.

Using both hands, Maple enthusiastically shoveled food into her mouth, her chubby cheeks moving as she ate.

"She likes it," Finley commented, watching Maple with a tender expression while she picked at her own food.

"It's good to see. And you?"

Finley nodded. "Yes, it's delicious, thank you." She took another dainty bite from her fork, her eyes still on Maple.

Those were the first kind words she'd said to me, but I wasn't going to bet that her sour streak was over.

The last time I'd seen her, she'd been dressed in all black, carrying a folded flag, tears rolling down her cheeks. She was a widow, way too young, and I'd been the one leading the mission that took Marcus from her. The guilt was insurmountable, so much so, that I spent all my free time pushing away everyone, working as much as possible, and chasing oblivion in the bottom of a bottle. She'd screamed at me in the parking lot that day, beat on my chest and dissolved into a puddle of tears. My SEAL teammates Nolan and West had carried her away, and I'd gotten into my truck, punching the steering wheel a few times trying to put physical pain into the anguish I felt inside.

I had a mountain of work to do if I ever wanted to bridge this gap between us. And there was no better time to start than now. But the last thing I wanted to do was stumble over a minefield...again. I had to approach this conversation carefully. Find some safe common ground. I couldn't talk about the weather—she'd instantly know that I had nothing else to say, which would just be pathetic. I couldn't think of any question about work that wouldn't come across as weird. She probably didn't have the spare time or cash for the theater, so unless I wanted to embarrass her, I couldn't ask whether she'd seen any recent movies.

"So, uh...how's your family?" I asked. Dammit, that was barely a step above the weather.

"They're okay. My mom retired a few years ago." She cocked a sharp eye at me. "In case you were wondering, no, I can't ask her to help me. She's on a fixed income."

"I wasn't going to suggest that," I protested.

Finley nodded and took another bite of food. I gave up the topic for dead. Maybe she and her mom weren't close.

But soon, in a much gentler tone, Finley added, "I'm afraid I don't have much else to say. My dad was never really around, and I'm bad about staying in touch with my mom's sister. Last I heard, she was getting divorced."

"Oh, that's too bad."

"Not really. My uncle was also kind of a bast...I mean, a huge jerk." Then she gave a flurry of quick blinks, as if she'd caught herself saying too much. "Uh, what about your family?"

I shook my head. "I'm not really close to them, either." One of the many features of being married to your job. Sometimes a pro, sometimes a con.

The noise of forks clinking against plates filled the room again. Talking about our relatives was pretty much a bust, but at least Finley had been willing. Hell, she'd even tried to throw me a bone. That was a promising sign.

Taking my time chewing, I dug through my memories of Finley from when I'd hung out with Marcus. She hadn't followed sports at all. Whatever her old job had been, that was likely a sore spot. But she'd had a hobby. Something ultra-feminine, like scrapbooking...only not that. Was it knitting? Fuck, I couldn't remember for sure. But I decided to take the chance.

"So, uh...do you still knit?" I asked.

Her eyebrows lifted slightly. "You remember that?"

Mentally pumping my fist in victory, I replied casually, "Yeah, of course."

"I don't have much time for it anymore, but occasionally..." The tiniest possible smile graced her lips. "While I watch TV with Maple."

I pictured them together: Finley perched on the couch, silver needles busily spooling out a bright wool scarf, with Maple sitting entranced between her knees. The homey image felt so warm it slowed my tense heartbeat.

Wait a second. I'm an idiot. Of course, there was a topic staring me right in the face. Every parent loves to talk about their children. "What shows does she like?"

"Well, we don't have cable—only Internet streaming—and I only let her watch educational stuff. So the selection's kind of limited." She actually chuckled a little. "Even though we never go over an hour a day, I swear I know all the songs somehow..."

Finley talked about Maple for the rest of dinner. It wasn't always riveting, exactly—only a parent could get passionate about stuff like potty training and fine motor skills. But the way Finley's face lit up with motherly love was more than enough reward for me. And Maple was having a great time; she grinned wide and wiggled in her high chair, knowing damn well that she was the center of attention. Cute little thing.

Halfway through dinner she instigated a game with me— making a squeal that I repeated back—over and over again.

"Are you through?" Finley asked, nodding toward my plate. I had a feeling she was going to kick me out immediately after dinner, but I nodded anyway.

I cleared the plates while she wiped Maple's hands and face. "I'm going to lay her down," Finley said, lifting a sleepy Maple into her arms.

Unsure what else to do, I started rinsing the dishes as the soft sounds of a lullaby drifted from down the hall.

About fifteen minutes later, Finley joined me in the living room, looking tired, and sunk down onto the worn sofa.

"Not what you expected of me?"

"Becoming a stripper? If I'm being honest, no." That was the last thing I would have ever guessed. Finley was soft spoken, reserved, with a quiet confidence and inner strength lurking under the surface. She wasn't flamboyant or overly sexual, or any of the other things you think of when you hear the word stripper.

"Sorry to disappoint you."

"You haven't," I corrected her. "I just want to help, and if I'm in a position to make your life a little easier, why not let me?"

"Because I don't accept handouts. I take care of what's mine," she said, an air of confidence to her voice.

"So do I." My tone matched hers and I sensed we were ready to square off, say all the things that had been kept bottled up for almost two years now.

"We'll never be yours, Greyson. Surely six years in the military under enemy fire didn't totally warp your brain."

I leaned in closer, and caught a whiff of vanilla and lavender. "That's the thing about SEALs – we're hard headed. And once that bond is formed, it's like a brotherhood – unbreakable."

God, were we ever. Marcus and I had been practically attached at the hip.

"So you're only doing this – looking in on us – to honor some memory?" Finley asked, pulling me from my somber thoughts.

"I didn't say that. If I didn't want to be here –I wouldn't." That was the absolute truth.

Her gaze studied mine, as if searching for the sincerity in my words, for my true motivation. Changing tactics, I tried for something more complimentary. "Seeing you last night brought up a lot of old memories, and meeting your little girl tonight – well she's amazing."

"Thank you." Finley blushed and lowered her chin again.

After several moments of stiff silence, she shifted on the couch, pulling her legs underneath her. "So what are you proposing?"

I was shocked that her defensiveness had softened so fast. But I squashed my pleasant surprise at the small victory. This couldn't possibly be that easy; I shouldn't let myself get too hopeful. Maybe she was just looking for more concrete ammunition to shoot down my offer. *Tread carefully, soldier.* "Let me come by. Allow me to help out. Surely there are things around the house that need done, things a man could help with."

She shook her head, frowning.

Damn stubborn woman.

"I'm sorry, I can't do that," she added.

I could see that it was more than that. Determination shined brightly in her eyes. The need to prove herself as a single working mother wasn't easy and she wanted, no, *needed* to prove she could make it.

I was going to let it drop. For now.

"I know you don't approve, but I have my reasons for working at the club."

I raised one brow. "And those would be …?"

"Dancing allows me to pay my bills, *mostly*, and still be home with my daughter during the day. Maple already lost her dad; I didn't want her mom to work fifty hours a week at an office an hour away and see her only at bedtime. She's all I have. And I'm all she has."

"I get that." I nodded.

"Besides that, daycare is expensive. A big chunk of whatever money I made from working days would go right back into a babysitter or daycare."

"Listen, I understand. You're providing for your daughter, I'm just saying I didn't like seeing you up there."

Finley smirked at me. "I'm sorry for your poor eyes...I know I'm a few years past my expiration date, not to mention I'm a mom now."

Past her expiration date? She had no fucking clue how wrong she was. I considered letting it go, but the way her eyes drifted down the floor and her fists closed tightly in her lap, I knew I had to set her straight. "That's not what I meant," I corrected her. "You were sexy as hell, and before I knew who you were, my cock was standing at attention, giving you a full salute."

Her cheeks went bright pink.

"Seriously," I said, "Where the hell did you learn moves like that?" I couldn't help the touch of respect in my voice.

"I can't believe you just told me you got hard …" She was still smirking at me and looking at me with a bit of wonder.

I shrugged. "We've been through too much to start beating around the bush now."

Beating. Bush. Those may have been the wrong choice in words. God, what was with me? I definitely didn't want her to know I'd gone home and jerked myself raw to thoughts of her naked breasts, tanned skin and silky curves.

She took a deep breath and released it slowly, her gaze lifting to mine. "When I'm on stage, it's the only place where I can really let myself go. The only time I'm free. I'm not a mom, not a grieving widow, I'm someone more fun, casual, and desirable. I guess I don't really think, I just feel the music and let it move me."

"Trust me, you're still very desirable." My throat felt tight, but I forced the words out. "You must do very well with tips," I added in an attempt to turn this conversation back to her profession and not her knockout body.

"No." She shook her head at the compliment. "I do okay. The location just off the highway makes for some cheap clientele – people just passing through. Especially the weeknight shifts, those are really slow."

My resolution to back off for now weakened. At the risk of sounding like a broken record, I took one last gamble. "I could help, Finley. You and Maple. I'm earning a good living, and with my retirement from the US Navy…"

I trailed off at the dead look in her lovely eyes. A dark, empty space carved out by grief, an anger so deep it had become a kind of exhaustion. It scared me what I saw there. I knew from personal experience the dark places your mind could go in those lowest moments.

"You can't buy forgiveness, Greyson," she said quietly, steadily. Too steady to be anything but holding back tears.

Her words sank between my ribs like cold, sharp steel. For a second, I couldn't remember how to breathe. *So this is what she really thinks of me…a murderer.*

It was nothing I hadn't yelled at myself every night for the past two years. The part that really felt like a kick in the balls was the idea that I was trying to pay off my guilt. Like all I wanted was permission to forget Marcus. When she put it that way, my offer sounded so…sleazy.

Before now, all her refusals had been grounded in her own

pride. *I can handle my own damn life my own damn way*, she'd insisted. And while I respected the hell out of that strength, I could still negotiate with it. Her real, unfiltered opinion of me...now that was entirely different. Nothing I said could ever change her feelings. She probably wouldn't even believe me if I tried.

.

"I know the damage is done." Resigned, I rose to my feet. This visit was long over. "I'm sorry it has to be this way. Let me know if you change your mind."

"I won't," she whispered as she closed the door behind me.

Chapter Four

Finley

"Ugh, he's out there again." I stood backstage, peeking from behind the velvet curtain and cursed under my breath.

"Who is, dear?" Ginger asked shuffling by me with a stack of freshly laundered towels.

Ginger was in her sixties, and was the unofficial *House Mom* of the club. She was the manager's stepmother and had a knack for looking after the girls. Her role was varied. Therapist, referee, makeup artist, hair stylist, schedule keeper, emergency seamstress, you name it, Ginger was on top of it.

But she was always here, and could always be counted on. She'd quickly become one of my favorite parts about working at the club.

"Brant freaking Rockwall." I made a grumbled sigh.

"That man has no life," Ginger remarked, setting a still-warm hand towel onto each girl's vanity.

"Yeah he does, it's called Watch Finley Like a Hawk." Layla said beside me.

"Gross," I muttered.

"Come back here and take a break. You don't have to go out there right now," Ginger said, patting the tufted chair in front of her desk.

"I do if I want to make some money tonight." As tempting as her idea sounded, I couldn't afford a break.

"Nonsense, you'll make plenty tonight. Let's just wait him out. Layla, go out there and tell him Stormy is gone for the night."

Stormy was my stage name. It wasn't something I'd put a lot of thought in to. When the manager asked me after my audition what I wanted to be called – I blurted the first word that popped into my head – and Stormy fit my mood exactly.

As Layla strutted out from backstage, obviously intent on telling Brant I was gone, I plopped down in the comfy chair in front of Ginger's desk. "Thanks for that." I guess I could sit for a few minutes while Layla got rid of Brant. Plus it was almost closing time, and I only had a few more songs to dance anyway.

She nodded. "Why don't you tell me what's really going on?"

For a moment, her question confused me. Then I realized she was talking about Grey, not Brant. *How the hell does she do that?* Ginger could always tell when one of her girls had trouble. Sometimes her spooky mind-reading ability was annoying, but her heart was in the right place, and her advice often helped.

I shrugged as nonchalantly as I could. "My husband's former combat partner, Greyson Archer came into the club the other day."

Her eyes widened. "And?"

"And he almost pulled me down off the stage."

Ginger smiled knowingly. "So he has a thing for you."

"No, of course not. Not like that. It's just his guilty conscience getting the best of him. He was the one with Marcus when …" I didn't continue, but I didn't need to. Ginger knew all the gory details. You couldn't keep much from her, and honestly I didn't even want to. She was a good listener, and often had insightful advice.

"Finley, dear, I hate to break this to you, but you're a very desirable woman. I'm not sure if you've thought about the future, but you can't stay single forever."

I held up one hand, stopping her.

"I'm not saying now is the time," she continued, her tone soft and coaxing, "I just think it'd be wise of you to consider that perhaps the man is interested."

I shook my head, and played with the gold bangles on my wrist. A nervous habit that I'd never managed to break. "For once, you're off the mark, Ginger. Grey's not interested in me like that ..."

Then I remembered what he said. That he'd been *excited* watching me dance. I quickly decided to ignore that. Men got excited watching strippers dance period. It was normal. It wasn't because it was *me*. In fact, Grey said that his cock had only stood at attention until he realized who I was. *Ouch.*

I frowned. Why was that thought so disappointing? It was never fun to hear that I'd killed someone's boner, but normally I wouldn't care about one single customer's opinion of my body.

Ginger held up her palms in a non-threatening gesture. I liked that she still wore her wedding ring so long after losing her husband. That was another thing we had in common. My own wedding band was now worn on my right ring finger instead of my left. My diamond solitaire I'd had to pawn months ago when my car broke down, but nothing would ever cause me to part with the simple gold band Marcus had slipped onto my finger that day in the church when he promised me forever.

"I'm just saying it wouldn't be the worst thing in the world to let yourself start having a little fun again. Explore the possibility of dating. Hell, even just sex might be nice." She smiled at me, her warm blue eyes crinkling in the corners.

"You did not just suggest I have a one-night stand with the man I told you is on my last nerve, did you?"

She reached over and patted my hand. "Just think about it."

Had the world gone entirely fucking crazy? First Greyson was expecting me to just take a handout, and now grandmotherly Ginger was telling me I needed to get laid? What was next? Afraid to find out, I rose to my feet and peeked out from the curtain. Seeing that Brant was now gone from the seat near the stage he generally commandeered, I headed over toward the DJ booth to request my song and prepare for my next dance.

***

An hour later, I was worn out and more than ready to get home to my little girl and warm bed. Rising up from my vanity stool on bare feet, I slipped on a hooded sweatshirt and my sneakers. My feet were sore from the stiletto heels I'd danced in all night and I almost moaned when my instep met the cushioned sole. Thank God for small pleasures. Most of the girls sat counting out their money at the end of the night, but I merely shoved mine in my purse.

Tonight had been a disaster – between Brant hanging around half my shift, and then my bra clasp deciding to stick mid-striptease, I was off my game tonight. Big time. I was sure it had nothing to do with Ginger telling me I needed to get laid. Yeah right. That wasn't on my agenda any time soon.

I was so glad when Layla stepped up to save me from anymore of Brant's unwelcome advances. My evening had gone a little smoother after that.

The club was now dark and quiet, and there were only a few of us left in the building. I grabbed my oversized purse, which often doubled as a diaper bag, and headed for the back exit. Our bouncer was waiting by the door, his beefy arms folded, watching as each girl filtered out in the darkened night.

"Night, Bruce," I said as I headed outside.

He gave me a nod and grunt, letting me know that nothing would happen to me where he could see it.

But the club's outdoor lights only reached so far. I was only three steps from my old beat-up Honda when Brant stepped out of the shadows.

Shit.

Glancing back toward the building, Bruce was nowhere in sight and the big steel door was already shut tight.

"Hey Finley."

I whipped around as a cold shiver raced through me. Blinking at him, I remained speechless as I tried to figure out how in the hell he found out my real name.

He let out a deep chuckle. "Your friend the other night, he called you that. It is your name, right?"

I swallowed hard. *Damn Greyson.* When he spotted me that night he must have said my name loud enough for the few people sitting nearby to hear.

"Uh...." I couldn't get my mouth and brain to cooperate.

He watched me with that creepy quiet smirk of his.

I didn't like him seeing *this* me. The *real* me. I'd scrubbed off most of my makeup with a wet wipe, and my hair was in a messy bun on the top of my head. It was one thing for him to be into me when I was in scene –I was every man's fantasy up on the stage, but it was something altogether different to have him standing here talking to me, not as a stripper and customer sharing an interaction, but as a man and woman. Panic prickled at the back of my neck, the skin raising up in goose bumps.

"They told me you went home, but your car was still here."

"So you waited," I deadpanned.

"Yeah, of course I did. Are you okay?"

I was avoiding you, you fuckwit.

"I'm fine. If you'll excuse me, it's been a long day, and I'm ready to get going."

"Of course, I understand." He smiled at me kindly and I thought maybe, just maybe it would be that easy to get rid of him. But then he stepped closer, and brought his hand up to my hairline. I backed away, taking two big steps back from my car. "Sorry." He smiled again. "It's just … you look younger with your hair up like that."

I didn't have it in me to be polite to him tonight. I wasn't working, wasn't trying to earn any tips. So even though he was smiling at me, I wasn't about to bat my eyelashes at the compliment. He didn't seem like the dangerous type, just lonely and a little weird, but I wasn't about to let my guard down now. I held my keys protectively in front of me, ready to strike out if necessary.

"I'm sorry for bothering you … I just wasn't ready to go home yet," he said, his voice softer.

He wore a wedding ring, for fuck's sake. *Go home to your wife.* If I was still married, I'd never be at a place like this looking to make a connection with a stranger.

Staring wistfully at my car, I was startled at the sound of Layla's voice.

"Is he bugging you again?" she asked, approaching us. I saw her car idling a few rows down and was so thankful she hadn't left yet.

"I've got it handled."

Brant chuckled and took a step back. "I don't mean any harm, ladies. I'll be on my way." He pulled a set of keys from his pocket. "Good night, Finley."

I didn't return his sentiment and he turned and headed to a silver sedan.

I heaved a sigh of sweet relief. "Thank God," I muttered into my hands.

Layla put a reassuring arm around me. "Listen, this has gone on long enough, we need to fix this."

"And what do you propose exactly?" If I complained to the management, I'd only get moved to the less desirable shifts or have my hours cut back even more than they already were. The club could only afford so many bouncers and if certain girls became targets for odd customers, I'd seen it handled that way before. I couldn't let that happen.

She leaned closer, her eyes narrowing. "I know a lady. She can put a curse on him. Make his small pecker shrivel up and fall off. You just have to bring her a chicken."

I almost laughed, until I saw in her eyes that she was completely serious. "No, it's okay, I'll be fine," I assured her. Somehow. It would have to be. I needed this job.

I said goodbye to Layla and got inside my car, watching her taillights fade into the distance. I sat there in the darkened interior, hands resting on the steering wheel, reflecting on the crazy last couple of days I'd had. As soon as Layla's car was gone from sight, a big black SUV pulled into the parking lot and came to a stop beside my car.

What now?

Greyson climbed out, looking upset about something.

I rolled down my window as he approached. I was still sore from our disastrous dinner, so I could have just driven off, but that would only give him an excuse to show up on my doorstep to check on me.

"Are you okay?" he asked, placing his hands on the door frame and leaning in.

"I'm fine," I lied. I didn't want him of all people knowing that a customer had just left me rattled.

Apparently his grief and guilt over Marcus made him want to play the role of white knight. It was so annoying how he always seemed to catch me at my worst. And of course, tonight was no different. I was exhausted, frustrated, and pretty sure there was black makeup smeared under my eyes. "What are you doing here?" I asked.

He shrugged. "I just had a strange feeling that something had happened."

I raised both eyebrows. I knew Greyson lived in the nice part of town, on the other side of the lake, a good twenty-minute drive. "So you drove up here?"

He nodded. "I figured you'd be getting off work. I knew the club closed at one."

The clock on my dash told me it was closer to two now, and getting up with Maple at six wasn't going to be fun. But I couldn't deny his strange sixth sense about me was proving to be spot on. "I was just about to head home."

"Was I right ... did something happen tonight?" he asked.

I gave a careful nod. "It's over now. Honestly, I'm fine."

"You've got to give me more than that, sweetheart." His tone left little room for negotiation.

"In this business there are some real creeps. I'm sure it was harmless. Just some misplaced affection."

Greyson's dark eyes stayed locked on mine for a few moments longer and I wondered if he was going to press me for the full story. Then he took a deep breath. "Are you sure you're okay?"

I nodded. "I just want to get home."

He dropped his hands and took a step back. "Okay, then. Goodnight."

"Night." Surprised that he wasn't going to argue with me like he had the other night, I cranked the engine and pulled out.

The shadowy hulk of his black SUV followed me out of the lot a minute later. I expected to see him turn at the corner towards the highway on-ramp. Instead, his headlights stayed in my rear-view mirror for mile after mile. It wasn't hard to keep track of him; at this unholy hour, so far out of town, we were the only two people on the road.

If any other guy had pulled this stunt, I'd already be calling 911. But I knew Greyson. He and Marcus had been friends for years. And even after Marcus died, even though I hated Grey for everything he'd taken away from me, I found I couldn't completely distrust him. Even if he was only helping me to soothe his own guilt, I could tell that his desire to help me was sincere in itself. He didn't have an ulterior motive—or rather, he did, but I knew it already. This was his attempt to atone for his sins, pure and simple. He hadn't gone to all this effort just to get into my pants or steal my kidneys or whatever the hell Brant was after. Grey's chivalry may have been annoying as hell...but it was pure. No funny business. *Unlike certain middle-aged creepazoids.*

So instead of pulling over to yell at him, I just kept driving. My new shadow followed me all the way to my dilapidated apartment complex. By the time I backed into my assigned parking spot, I was surprised to find tears in my eyes. As much as I resented Grey, nobody had shown such genuine concern for me in a long time. Nobody else had cared whether I got home safely.

I turned off the engine, stepped out, and saw him idling in the middle of the narrow lot. I almost wanted to wave goodbye. Almost.

He finally roared away when I shut the front door behind me. I walked through my silent apartment, finding the babysitter asleep in the armchair. I shook her shoulder to wake her and handed her some of the cash I'd just made. And then she was gone, and I was alone again. I breathed in the thick, musty stillness as I slipped off my shoes.

I crept into the bathroom to wash my face, but something made me pause just before I turned on the water. I stared blankly into the mirror. The remnants of the makeup I wore for every shift was left, and I knew the customers loved it. But in that moment, my face struck me as a grotesque mask. Bloody lips, porcelain skin, cartoonish lashes, eyeliner and shadow smeared into bruise-blue raccoon circles. This wasn't me. This was barely even a woman. This was a...plaything.

My insides tightened, all the way from my stomach to my throat. My eyes burned from more than the makeup. What was I doing here? Who *was* I? What had my life become?

Stifling a sob, I hurried into Maple's nursery. I needed the comfort of her sweet little snores, her clean milky smell, the sight of her tiny hand curled in her mouth. Some reminder that I wasn't really as alone as I felt. Some reassurance that everything—the grief, the long hours, the lack of sleep, the humiliation—would all be worth it in the end.

But it wasn't enough. I sank down beside her crib and cried as quietly as I could. I hated myself for surrendering to hysteria like this. I hated how deep Grey's stormy eyes always saw into my soul. I hated the fact that he might be the only man in the world who could understand me. The only other person who ached so much over the same loss.

Chapter Five

Greyson

It had been a long fucking day. Between lack of sleep after I'd escorted Finley home in the middle of the night, to dealing with a tough assignment at work all day, I was ready for a drink. Arriving home, I tossed my keys and cell phone onto the kitchen counter and made my way straight to the dark walnut and leaded glass liquor cabinet. I'd bought this thing from an estate sale and restored it myself, sanding and staining the wood and replacing the old cracked glass. Now it held expensive bottles of various liquors that I rarely indulged in. But days like today? You bet your ass I'd be enjoying at least a few.

Dropping a couple of ice cubes into the bottom of a tumbler, I added a long pour of Glenmorgie. It wasn't the world's best Scotch – by far – but it was what my dad used to drink when he was still alive, and something about the golden bottle and the stiff, smoky aroma conjured up pleasant memories.

My house, while it was quiet and tidy, felt lacking. Ignoring the strange feelings stirring inside me, I settled down onto the couch and flipped on the TV just for some background noise. Then I took a calming sip of my drink.

I'd bought this house within a week of retiring from the SEALs. It was too big for just a bachelor, but the two-story brick structure with its wide front porch made a statement. I hadn't put too much thought into it; tired of moving around, I'd just wanted somewhere permanent, so I'd let my gut choose this place for me. At the time, with military life fresh in my memory, this house had felt right. I wasn't going anywhere, wasn't going to spend anymore sleepless nights on a cot in the desert with a loaded gun at my side, and there was comfort in that.

But as I sat here now, I realized that my once-refuge was too quiet, even with the TV blaring. It was too big and empty. It was strange how I felt more comfortable in Finley's tiny apartment filled with laughter and squeals than I was in my own home.

Finley... I took another sip of whiskey, larger this time. I both wanted and didn't want to think about her. The tangle of pain that tied us together.

To all outside appearances, I'd moved on. I'd retired from the military, bought a house in a quiet suburb north of Dallas, started working as a consultant for a private security firm run by my former commander. I had settled into a picture-perfect civilian routine. But actually getting on with my life - forgiving myself for what happened, finding pleasure in my newfound freedom? I wasn't there yet. And now, knowing how Finley was living, letting go of the past just wasn't an option.

The memories of her that had been etched into my brain needed to change. All I saw when I looked at her was the way she'd looked at the funeral, screaming and sobbing, the tears of anger and desperation sliding down her cheeks. I wanted to paint over that memory with something more positive. Like watching her with her daughter. Marcus would've been wrapped around his little girl's finger. Didn't matter that he was a two-hundred pound SEAL—Maple had a way about her.

I could tell then that Finley had been pregnant. Maybe it was a sixth sense. Maybe it was the way her hand absently went to her belly. Whatever it was that cued me in, I'd looked closer, and seen the slight swell under her black wrap dress that had never been there before. She obviously wasn't telling people yet, so I hadn't said anything. I figured it was either too early to share the news, or just that the somber occasion wasn't the place she wanted to do it.

Shit, looking back now, I realized that she'd been just barely pregnant, yet already holding her almost-flat belly. Protectively, fearfully, in a silent show of worry for the difficult life ahead of her. She'd known exactly how hard single motherhood would be. No time to grieve and find closure—her attention had been forced towards the future. I'd never pieced that all together before now. Just another reason why I was determined to make sure she wouldn't have to go it alone.

I'd tried for years to act like I was immune to her, like I didn't notice special things about her, but I knew them all. The small, crescent-shaped birthmark at the nape of her neck that only showed when she wore her hair up. The way the gold bangle bracelets she favored hung on her slender wrist. Delicate fingers that she kept painted pink, or red, or something equally girly at all times. Of course I'd noticed the change in her that day. But I'd tried like hell to disappear and stay out of her way, since I was probably the last person she wanted to see – a constant visual reminder of her loss.

Letting out a heavy sigh, I considered driving down to my buddy West's bar for a drink, maybe picking up a woman to bring home and keep me company for the night. Filling my bedroom with the sounds of flesh slapping against flesh and feminine cries of pleasure would be better than sitting here, so deep in silence that the hum of the refrigerator almost deafened me.

But of course, whoever I picked up wouldn't be the one I really wanted. Finley … with her sweet curves, and green eyes, and sassy attitude that made me work for every inch of ground I gained with her.

Fuck.

Why was I sitting here thinking about Finley like *that?* She was my buddy's widow. End of fucking story. If there was one thing that flowed through my veins, it was honor. Poaching her after his death would be unforgiveable. Truly putting the final nail in his coffin.

But I hadn't even thought about anyone else in the days since I'd first run into her. Hell, I'd jacked myself raw every night to the memory of her up on that stage. Eyes closed – grinding her hips – blonde hair flowing like a halo. Her body was built for sin, but there was something angelic about her, too. Maybe it was because I knew she was a sweet mother to a little girl. Or it could have been the pure white lace delicately covering up all the parts of her I wanted to taste. Those rosy pink nipples, the soft folds between her creamy thighs …

I cursed under my breath and rose from the couch. I needed to stop this line of thinking right now. Even if a future was possible with Finley, she'd never think of me that way. Not after how Marcus had died. *That* much was obvious from how things had gone down at our last dinner. The best I could do now would be to stay out of her way and offer up subtle help with her little girl in a way she couldn't refuse.

I owed it to everyone involved—myself, Marcus, Finley, and Maple—to at least try. Grabbing my cell phone, I hit the contact number for my boss, Jerry.

"Everything okay?" he answered. He knew today's assignment had been a shitstorm, but that wasn't what was occupying the space in my brain.

"Yeah. It's fine. I was actually calling about something else. Something … *personal.*"

He was quiet for several seconds. He and I didn't do the personal sharing thing. "O-kay?" He drew out the word, obviously at a loss as to what the fuck I was going to spring on him.

"I wanted to let you know that I won't be in tomorrow."

"What's going on? Are you sure everything's alright?"

I'd never missed a day of work. Not even when I had the stomach flu last year. But after relying on the trash can under my desk as a sick-basin, my team had kicked me out of the office. Rightly so. That had been my one and only absence while working for Redstone.

"It will be. It's Finley Sutton, Marcus's widow." I cleared my throat, feeling strangely choked up. "She needs some help."

"I see. Is there anything I can do?" he asked.

"I don't think so. I've got it covered." I could have asked him for just about anything, and he would have helped in an instant. But this duty was mine to fulfill.

"Of course. Take all the time you need," Jerry said before we ended the call. He knew my history with Marcus, and therefore the level of responsibility I felt toward his widow. I knew he wouldn't argue with me, but still it felt good to get it out in the open.

Jerry had a streak of loyalty that ran even deeper than mine. And several months ago, when his daughter Lacey had been kidnapped, I had been every bit as committed to her rescue as Nolan had. Jerry would just have to do without me for one day.

***

The next afternoon, Finley stared at me through the crack in the doorway. I could only see one green eye watching me through the small space, but it still sent a small jolt through me.

"Hey," I offered. Obviously we weren't on friendly terms, despite my efforts lately.

"Hey," she returned, voice cold and emotionless.

"Can I … come in?"

She let out a deep, exasperated sigh. "Did you need something?"

"Just to talk." I held up both palms in a show of innocence.

She shut the door abruptly, and I heard the chain slide free from the lock before she pulled it open again. "Talk, Greyson." Now that I had a full view, I saw that Finley was dressed in an oversized sweatshirt that fell off one shoulder, exposing a black bra strap, and a pair of well-fitted jeans that clung to her rounded hips and ass. I didn't *want* to notice things like this about her—fuck, I wasn't even sure I wanted to be here on her doorstep, but something bigger than me was at work here. I was compelled. And so here I was.

When I finally tore my gaze away from her, I could see Maple playing on the living room floor. She looked up at me and smiled. "Ay-son," she said in that sweet little voice that could melt a man faster than the Texas sun.

"Hi, angel."

"So ..." Finley prompted.

I resisted the urge to tilt my head to the side and pop my neck, despite the headache I could feel building. *Focus, Grey.* She might not like me, but her daughter did. I had to use every angle to my advantage.

"I know we've talked about this, and you made it very clear where you stand. But I have a proposition for you. Let me be here for *her.*" I tipped my chin toward Maple.

She narrowed her eyes on mine. "Why would you want to do that?"

I knew she was thinking this was some strange brotherhood-bond thing, but it was more than that. Something inside me just wanted to be around them. It made me feel ... *normal.* It gave my life some much needed spice. "She needs a father figure in her life, Finley. It'll be good for her."

She made a little *hmpf* sound in her throat, but she didn't argue. She couldn't, because she knew I was right, even if it was only about that one thing.

And from that point forward, I started coming twice a week, like clockwork. On Tuesdays and Thursdays, I'd bring dinner by and hang out with Maple for a couple of hours before bedtime. We read stories, played make-believe, fed her baby doll from a spoon, and watched cartoons on my iPhone while she curled in my lap.

I didn't change diapers, didn't try to play the hero, and I definitely didn't try to engage Finley in any deep or meaningful conversations. But it worked. Slowly things started to become less awkward. Slowly I felt the walls that Finley had constructed around her and her daughter begin to slip. And the knots of tension that had trapped us in place began to unravel.

And today, three weeks later, here I was again, pulling up to the apartment with a bag of groceries. Only this time, in addition to the takeout, I had a bottle of red wine tucked inside the bag too. I hadn't pushed Finley for more, hadn't pressured her again about quitting the club, but of course it had been lurking in the back of my mind. Tonight, I planned to give her a gentle nudge.

"Chinese?" Finley asked with skepticism, removing the white cartons from the bag and setting them on the table.

"A man can only eat so much macaroni and cheese." I

grinned at her. Usually I opted for getting Maple's favorite foods, but tonight I wanted to try something different. Fuck, I needed to if my taste buds were to survive. "There's fried rice and egg rolls and a few other things, hopefully that's okay." I shifted Maple to my other arm. When I was here, she often clung to me like a little koala bear, which Finley assured me was not the norm. She didn't go to strangers, didn't let just anyone hold her. Which of course made me feel like the luckiest man in the world. She trusted me. Her mom, on the other hand … I was pretty sure I'd moved only from lurid hatred to mild irritation on her barometer.

Finley's tone softened. "This is perfect. I didn't want to complain, since I know you've been making such an effort, but I don't think I could have eaten another bite of macaroni."

I chuckled at her, but my laughter stopped short when I saw her holding up the bottle of wine with a look of confusion etched into her pretty features. Since I'd been coming here, I hadn't done anything remotely romantic, nothing to suggest our time together was a date. No, I was here for Maple. Plain and simple. But the wine, the non-toddler food—it was different than my usual MO, and she picked up on it right away.

"Merlot?" she asked, inspecting the bottle. It wasn't expensive, but it wasn't cheap either.

"What? Does French wine not pair well with Chinese? I

can never remember these things."

She made one of those *hmpf* noises I was coming to know meant she was annoyed, but wasn't going to argue. Then she set the bottle down. "I'll look for my wine opener. It's been a while since I used it."

Interesting. Not only was she not going to fight me, she was going to indulge in a glass with me. It felt like a small victory, but a victory nonetheless.

I fixed Maple's pink princess plate while Finley poured the wine.

She set our plates out while Maple dug in. I grabbed the sippy cup of milk in the fridge. It wasn't lost on me that Finley's routine had expanded to include me. Despite her reluctance about letting me into their life, we had gotten into a comfortable groove, our interactions slowly becoming less awkward and more sincere.

As we took our first bites, Maple was still busy inspecting her food with chubby toddler fingers. When she picked up the egg roll and shoved a big bite into her mouth, Finley's eyes lifted to mine and we both let out a laugh.

After dinner, I decided to hang around while Finley gave Maple her bath. Usually this was the time I'd cut out and leave them to their mother-daughter evening routine. But we still had a mostly full bottle of Merlot, and so I decided to test her. It was now or never. I refilled both our glasses, and was waiting on the couch when Finley reemerged from the hallway.

"Oh." She stopped in her tracks. "You're still here."

Ouch. Maybe Maple loved me, but her mother sure didn't.

After all the hours I'd invested trying to win Finley over, it was clear that I was still sitting at square one.

"Sorry, I'll ..." I made a move to stand.

But Finley crossed the room to place one hand on my shoulder. "I'm sorry. I didn't mean it like that. You don't have to rush off." She closed her eyes and took a deep breath to steady herself, then slowly pulled her hand away. "God, I've been a total bitch to you. It's just that ..."

"It's okay. I get it, alright? Don't beat yourself up." She was still healing, still grieving, and I knew she was doing the best she could. "Come sit down for a minute."

She did, pulling her legs up underneath her and accepting the wine glass I handed her.

"Maple really likes you," she said, taking a sip.

"Yeah, she's pretty sweet." Never thought I'd be a kid type

of guy, but she was just so damn cute.

As Finley settled in beside me, the scent of vanilla and soap greeted me. I took another long sip of wine, hoping to tramp down the feelings of lust she stirred in me.

"Have you kept in touch with any of the other guys? Nolan? West?" she asked.

I grunted an affirmative. "Yeah. West owns the bar in town now. He totally remodeled the place. It's doing quite well."

"Is he still a surly son of a bitch?" She smirked at me.

I barked out a short laugh. "That's not how I would have put it, but yeah, sure is. He needs a good woman in his life. His ex really did a number on him."

"Scarlet, right?"

"Good memory."

Finley shrugged. "She actually used to work at the club. She was gone by the time I started, but I've heard some pretty unsavory stories."

"I bet. I knew that girl was trouble from the first time I laid eyes on her. Manipulative. Opportunistic." Made my fucking stomach turn, just thinking of all the ways she fucked him up. But cheating on him when he was deployed was by far the worst.

"I promise not all the girls at the club are like that. For the most part, they're nice, normal women."

"Like you?" I asked.

She nodded and took another sip of her wine, her eyes cast down on the floor.

Clearing my throat, I continued on. "Nolan's settled down, found himself a woman who can handle all his shit. Lacey." Just saying her name made me happy. She really was Nolan's perfect match. The light to his occasional dark, stormy moods. Which reminded me—I owed them a visit. It had been too long.

"That's good to hear," Finley agreed.

"What about you?" I asked. "You keep in touch with anyone from the old crew?"

"No, I admit I haven't done a good job at that. Aside from Marcus's parents."

"They still live in Florida?"

She nodded. "Yes. I do video chats with them so they can see Maple grow. I don't think she quite gets it yet, she usually just tries to chew on my phone. And they're great about sending little gifts and seeing her when they can. They don't know about the money issues," she admitted softly.

"And you? How have you been, really?" Despite the times

we'd spoken recently, I still didn't think I'd gotten to the truth of how she was faring. Tonight I wanted to strip away all of the pretenses and get to the heart of the situation that had haunted me for almost two years.

Her fingers on the stem of the glass trembled. "How do you think? My husband was killed. I had a baby – alone. None of that was ever in my life plan."

"But you managed."

"I did." Her eyes flashed with determination, despite all she'd been forced to endure. It was something I admired about her big time. In my line of work, weakness could get you killed. Staying clear-headed and focused and just doing what you had to do to survive were deeply ingrained in me. And Finley spoke the same language.

"Why are you looking at me like that?" She lifted one manicured eyebrow at me, a smirk pulling up her lips.

"I'm impressed – how you've held it all together. How you're raising Maple alone."

She shrugged off the compliment. "It's what I had to do. And it's what anyone would have done in my shoes."

"It's not what everyone would have done," I corrected her. A weaker person would have sought comfort at the bottom of a bottle, or worse.

"You're incredible. In so many ways."

"I'm a damn stripper, for Christ's sake, Greyson. Listen to yourself. You make it sound like I'm Mother Theresa. I take my clothes off for money and shake my tits in their face."

"That's what I'm telling you, you don't have to be a stripper. You can be whatever you want to be." I'd seen the strength, determination, and just sheer bullheadedness she possessed. There was no doubt in my mind she'd tackle any obstacle flung her way.

"And what would you have me be, Grey? The pretty little wife to a man from my somber past?"

Adrenaline shot through me, making my heart pump faster and my hands curl into fists.

"I couldn't live with myself," she added under her breath.

Taking a chance, I slid closer to her on the couch and lifted my fingertips to her cheek. Her skin was even softer than it looked – and warm.

"That's not what I was implying at all. But I *could* be here for you. Not just for Maple, but to take care of you." I smoothed my thumb across her skin. She closed her eyes, and leaned slightly into my touch.

But then her eyes flashed open. "I can take care of myself."

"I know you can. But I'm assuming you haven't had a man in your life in a long time … someone to count on, someone to …"

Her gaze penetrated mine and the words died in my throat. *To what?* Pleasure her body? Give her a few mind-blowing orgasms? If I said it out loud, I knew I'd sound like an ass, so I didn't. I just continued stroking her velvety soft skin and watched as her breathing grew shallow.

I took the glass of wine from her hand and set it on the coffee table next to mine. "Come here," I murmured, pulling her close. Lowering my mouth to hers, I kissed her softly. She tasted sweet from the wine and her full lips parted, granting me access to sweep my tongue along hers. A bolt of desire shot down my spine and hardened my cock.

My hand slid down from her cheek to the column of her throat, where I could feel the insistent thumping of her pulse. Her tongue tangled with mine in desperate, hungry sweeps. Everything about this moment seemed surreal, from the soft little sighs in the back of her throat to her soft yet eager lips. My cock pressed painfully against my zipper, making me aware of just how badly I wanted her.

I wanted to pin her down against the couch, feel her body moving under mine, the tilt of her hips to meet my powerful thrusts. I wanted to hear the breathy cries that were sure to fall from her lips. Instead, I continued exploring her mouth, my hands cradling her jaw.

"Stop." Finley pulled back, her lips swollen and her eyes soft with arousal. But her tone was all wrong. She looked confused and upset.

My cock had grown rock hard, but my arousal died instantly at the word stop. I respected her need for space and pulled back, putting several inches between us. "What's wrong?"

"It's just that ..." Her gaze drifted over to where her late husband's portrait rested on the bookshelf.

I remembered that day like it was yesterday, despite the fact it was about seven years ago. We'd all been outfitted in our service dress blues and told not to smile. That didn't stop Marcus, though. His grin was wide and bright and his blue eyes shone back at us. Looking at it now sent an eerie feeling creeping over me.

Glancing back at Finley, I saw an uneasy look had settled across her features. "My daughter's asleep in the other room," she said finally.

"I understand." Hell, I didn't want to rush things either, and I was ready to combust if we kept up much longer. She was just starting to come around and I didn't want to push her too far too fast. There were so many delicacies to this situation that needed to be considered. "I should go."

She nodded. "Yes, that's probably a good idea."

Was her willpower hanging by a thread like mine was?

"Okay," I said, rising from the couch and headed toward the front door. With Finley trailing behind me, I discreetly adjusted my erection, angling it to the left of my thigh so I could fucking walk.

"You can come and see Maple since you get along so well, but that's as far as it can go," she added, sounding more firm.

When we reached the threshold to the door, I couldn't resist the temptation of pulling her close. A gentle hug was what I intended, nothing more. "Whatever you want," I murmured.

She lifted her eyes to mine and without hesitation, I pressed my lips to hers again and suppressed a groan at how good she tasted. Finley might have told me we had to stop, but that didn't prevent her from rubbing herself against me, pushing her hips into mine. She gasped when she felt what she'd done to me. And when I ground back against her, she groaned in frustration.

She pulled back again, almost as if she was pained by this whole exchange. With her eyes locked on mine, we both fought to catch our breath. Chests heaving, we just stood there, watching each other.

We'd never done anything remotely like this, but I'd always

been attracted to her, and I wondered if she was attracted to me, too. It had been a long damn time since I'd gotten any. I'd had no interest in chasing pussy while I'd been looking after Fin and Maple.

Tearing myself away, I drew a deep breath. My entire body was throbbing with need. Finley chewed on her lower lip, struggling with something internally. But what, I didn't know. Her desire for me as a woman desires a man? Or was she interested in something more? Some deep, messy entanglement that I'd always sworn I didn't need. But the mere idea of something more ... something *real nipped* at me, tearing tiny holes in my armor. Coming home to baby squeals and goodnight stories and a woman who was so strong, yet so soft. ...

No, I couldn't let myself go there. I was only coming here to care for my best friend's family, to set right what I'd done wrong. She wasn't meant to be mine. *They* weren't meant to be mine.

But that didn't stop me from picturing it. From wanting it so badly it fucking hurt.

I tucked a stray lock of hair behind her ear. "Not like this."

She gave a tiny nod.

"Lock up behind me, okay?"

"I will."

"And call if you need anything."

"I will," she echoed, her voice whisper soft.

"Night, baby."

"Night."

It was all wrong. But I couldn't stop myself from thinking that maybe, just maybe...this was a start.

I'd driven halfway home before I realized that I'd called her *baby*.

Chapter Six

Finley

"You want to take her where?" I crossed my arms over my chest, narrowing my eyes. This was not what I'd expected to hear when I opened my door first thing in the morning.

Grey shrugged. He had brought a tiny pink fishing pole as a gift for Maple. "What's wrong with catfishing?"

"Just making sure I heard you right. A toddler, fishing? Are you out of your mind? Hooks and deep water and..."

"Hickory Lake is just a small, shallow neighborhood pond. It's *meant* for little kids. And this thing doesn't even take a hook, only a plastic bobber." He reached out to rest his hand on my shoulder. "Trust me, Fin. I'll watch her like a hawk. I'd sooner die than let anything happen to her."

Trying to ignore the warmth of his touch, I studied his face closely. But I couldn't find a trace of insincerity in his expression—only a pure, fatherly fondness. He was dead serious about protecting Maple.

"Ay-son!" Maple toddled over to him at top speed and glued herself to his leg.

"Why, good morning, sweetheart." He bent down to greet her. She grabbed his proffered pinky, staring up at him with a wide, gummy grin.

Jesus, this level of adorable ought to be illegal. Why did he have to be so sweet with her? Just because Maple thought Grey walked on water didn't mean I should turn into a gooey puddle. No amount of corny Hallmark moments could change the fact that my husband was dead. It should be Marcus standing here, holding Maple's tiny hand, giving her presents and taking her out on daddy-daughter dates.

Even knowing all that, though, Grey's gentle smile still calmed my heart...and touched off a spark in my belly. And that kiss from last night didn't help. I shook off the sexy mental images just as Grey looked up again.

"So how about it?" he asked, eyebrows raised slightly in encouragement. "I'm betting you haven't had a real day off in a while." He handed me a gift card for a local spa. "Go get a massage or whatever it is women like to do."

Maple switched her pleading gaze to me. Her huge green eyes were a weapon of mass cuteness and she knew it. And a day at the spa sounded like heaven.

I melted immediately. "Okay," I said before I could think better of it. "I do need something..." My job forced me to keep up with leg and bikini waxes, but my hair was getting too long, and my feet were dying for some TLC after dancing in high heels every damn night.

I showed Grey how to attach the child seat into his car, then drove downtown to Roxy's Locks and booked a haircut and deluxe pedicure. I sank into the padded salon chair. As the wispy attendant fluttered and fussed over me, I started to relax. The constant mental refrain of work and worries, time and money, gradually faded away. But in the resulting quiet, I could hear all the questions I'd been avoiding. Life was so busy, so full of moment-by-moment demands, that it had been easy to keep my mind off the big picture. I had taken that excuse gratefully. Now, however, I was all alone with my thoughts—and they always found their way back to Grey.

I closed my eyes, tears threatening. I wondered what on earth Marcus would think of all this. Would he judge me and think this was totally wrong? Or would he be happy that a man he loved and trusted was taking care of us?

I'd been so scared to even consider a future with another man. I'd thought it would feel like a betrayal. Either he wouldn't measure up to Marcus...or he would, and I'd feel traitorous, tricked by my own heart into breaking our wedding vows. But I'd come to realize that nothing I did could ever damage our marriage. Death had done us part—those days with Marcus were far behind me. And though I would never, could never forget a single moment, I wondered if my heart did have room for more. I needed reason to smile again. Maybe Grey and Marcus didn't sully or overshadow each other. They represented totally different parts of my life. And dear God, I wanted to actually enjoy my life again.

I said a silent prayer begging Marcus to understand.

Please.

Please help me see what I'm supposed to do.

"Miss?" The pedicurist asked, bringing me back to reality. "Is this the color you wanted?" She held up a bottle of baby pink polish.

"Yes, thank you."

I watched as she painted carful strokes of polish over my buffed toes and my thoughts drifted to Greyson again.

The longer he came over to our place, the more normal it had felt. At first, I'd only let him play with Maple while I watched, eagle-eyed, skeptical that a never-married soldier boy could handle a toddler. But eventually I let his duties expand: feeding her at dinner, brushing her hair, wiping her face, entertaining her while I relaxed in a hot bath. And in return, our routine expanded to include him. I started taking it for granted that he'd show up twice a week, like clockwork, bearing dinner and a few precious hours of respite.

Before I knew it, three weeks had passed. Six visits. Dozens of deli boxes of mac 'n cheese for all of us, countless bedtime stories and peekaboo games for Maple...and then, at last, one bottle of Merlot. For me.

This arrangement wasn't supposed to be about me. The only way I could swallow my pride and let myself accept Grey's help was by making it all about Maple. Her learning to say his name had been the straw that broke my back. *Oh, screw it,* I'd thought, *Maple likes the bastard for some reason, and I shouldn't deprive her of a father figure just because she's got terrible taste in men.* She deserved a better childhood than the one I could give her on my own. And it was only for a little while, just until I could get on my feet. I furiously denied that my choice had anything to do with Grey himself—his handsome face, his broad shoulders and tight ass, his gentle but firm insistence on taking care of us. The most I'd ever admit was how refreshing it was to talk with someone who knew more than three words.

So I'd let him into our life. We didn't talk directly to each other much, apart from quick questions like "where's the paper towels?" But the atmosphere was still comfortably domestic. I'd never expected to feel that way again. With any man, let alone Greyson fucking Archer.

I almost wished I could feel more awkward. I was practically playing house with my husband's executioner. So why did the sight of him bring a smile to my face and loosen the tension in my shoulders? He made me feel like everything was going to be okay. Even though he'd been the one who made my life not-okay in the first place.

But when he brought the wine and Chinese takeout, I'd been shocked to find my pride still dormant. It all seemed so...natural. This was just the next step, something that came as easily as exhale followed inhale.

Usually Grey showed himself out as soon as Maple's bedtime rolled around—or I kicked him out. But late night, while Maple slept, we'd lingered together. Less than an hour on my ratty sofa. *No big deal*, I'd convinced myself. After almost a month of visits, Greyson was something like a friend, and friends shared a glass of wine all the time. Right? And I hadn't exactly been nice to him up until that point. I'd figured I should stop freezing him out and try to meet him halfway.

And then...

I had no idea what the hell had happened. One moment, we'd been sitting at a polite distance, and then we were kissing. And it happened again at the door—so much more than a chaste goodbye kiss. Just the memory made heat flutter between my thighs. His erection had ground into me and I had responded so shamelessly, rubbing against him. I hadn't felt like that in years. Like a real live woman. Like when I danced on stage, flying free, music flowing vibrant through my veins—only so much better. I'd almost forgotten that my body could bring me such pleasure.

But dammit, why did it have to be with *him*? How could I let myself do that? All the guilt and confusion I'd felt about Grey playing father to Maple...now it was a hundred times worse. I was cheating on Marcus's memory.

Now that he'd touched me, though, I couldn't stand the idea of never feeling him again. Our little makeout session had been more than hot—it had felt *right*. I couldn't deny that Grey woke me up in ways that I'd thought were long dead. Buried right along with Marcus. Even now, I wanted him.

So what the hell was I going to do? Could I bring myself to nip this in the bud? Or...

I tried to clear my head and focus on the pedicure. It almost worked.

***

When I returned, the table was full – a steaming plate of hot dogs, a bowl of baked beans, and a salad for two. Grey was in the process of wrangling Maple into her high chair. Her pink princess plate was already on the tray and loaded with a cut-up hot dog and a dollop of beans.

"You made this?" I asked as I took off my shoes.

His mouth quirked. "What, you think a grown man can't cook hot dogs?"

"No, it's just..." Grey had always brought some kind of takeout. Him buying groceries and cooking us a meal, even a simple one, felt so much more fatherly. *Homey.* Like he was a real part of our small, strange family. I shook my head. "Never mind. Thanks for dinner."

Maple got almost as much food in her mouth as on her face, which I hailed as a success. After we were done eating, I gave Maple her bath, dressed her in her favorite lamb jammies, and tucked her into bed with her stuffed owl. I came out of her nursery to find all the dishes washed and Greyson sitting on the couch...with two glasses of Merlot on the coffee table.

Was he hoping for this to become a new routine? I should have just kicked him out like usual. If I'd been quicker on the draw. If I hadn't been so grateful for the unexpected holiday. If he weren't so goddamn handsome. If last night's kisses hadn't seared right through me.

Instead, I sat down next to him and took a sip of wine. Who knows? Maybe my body understood what was right for me, even if I hadn't realized it yet.

"So how was Hickory Lake?" I asked.

He chuckled, the corners of his eyes crinkling. "It was fun. I taught her to cast, and she sat right next to me and pretended to fish. We were there until about noon."

"She actually sat still for that long? No way." I enjoyed the mental image of them perched side-by-side on the shore, like a pair of old men.

"Of course not. She was very busy...wanted to look at all the frogs and weeds and everybody else's catches. I hardly had a moment to catch anything myself."

I smiled, a tender warmth welling up inside me. Fishing wasn't really my thing, but Grey painted such an idyllic picture that I almost wished I'd come along with them.

As if Grey had read my mind, he looked straight into my eyes. "I've never seen you smile like that," he murmured.

My mind went blank. The moment held its breath as I tried to come up with a reply. But I couldn't think with Grey's gaze on me. Just sitting next to this man made me feel loose and floaty, like I was drunk after barely half a glass. But I knew it wasn't the wine that had done this to me. I had tasted Grey last night—and I wanted more.

Was it him or me who edged closer? Who had made the first move? Everything was such a blur. Without my realizing it, we had been poised like magnets on a table, just distant enough to stay apart. At the slightest nudge—his hand brushing mine, my tongue poking out to wet my lips—we flew to slam together.

Our mouths devoured each other. His arms enveloped me, one hand tangled in my hair, the other tight around my waist, already pushing up my shirt. Need flared down my spine. I wanted Grey to rip my clothes off and fuck me hard, right there on the sofa. My desire ached so intensely it almost scared me. I clutched at him, feeling his strong muscles, the amazing body that was so close to giving me what I craved. My eyes fluttered with anticipation...

And I glimpsed the photo of Marcus, so handsome in his SEAL dress blues, that hung on the living room wall. Watching everything.

My late husband's disappointed stare washed ice straight down my veins, cooling any heat I felt. I shoved Grey away, panicked, disgusted with myself, hot shame burning through me.

"Finley?" He looked confused. And just as rock-hard as before.

I tore my eyes away from the huge bulge in his jeans. "Y-you should go."

He blinked, forehead creased. "Why? What's wrong?"

"It's just...it's best if you go." *Please*, I added silently. *Before my willpower runs out.*

He gave me a long, careful look, but I kept my eyes trained on the floor. "All right," he finally said.

I didn't get up as he put on his coat and shoes. He could see his own infuriatingly tight ass to the door. The last thing I wanted—oh God, the only thing I wanted—was a repeat of last night.

But he paused with his hand on the doorknob and I tried not to growl with frustration. "Would it be okay if I come see Maple this Saturday? I know it's not our usual thing, but I saw something on TV about a special aquarium show, and she loved the fish today, so—"

"No," I said more sharply than I meant to. "She'll be in Florida all weekend. My in-laws are coming to get her." Some ugly voice inside me, something I didn't like at all, prompted me to add, "She'll be visiting Marcus's family."

I instantly regretted emphasizing that detail. It was cruel and totally unnecessary. But Grey only nodded, his expression unruffled, as if I hadn't just tried to cut his heart out. "Sure thing," he said. "Maybe next weekend."

Grey shut the front door quietly to avoid waking Maple. I buried my face in the couch's threadbare pillow, unable to meet Marcus's somber eyes. Grey's touch still burned under my skin.

Chapter Seven

Greyson

The information that Finley had given me – that Maple would be out of town visiting her grandparents – played through my brain all week. Not just because I wouldn't get to see Maple this week, but because it meant Finley would be alone, child-free, and able to spend some adult time with me. By Friday at lunch, I couldn't take the suspense any longer. I needed to know her schedule. Needed to know if there was any hope of seeing her. The last time at her place only made me more desperate for her. To show her all the ways we could make this work and heal together.

Parking my SUV in a spot near the club entrance, I killed the ignition and headed inside. My eyes took a moment to adjust to the dim lighting, and my nostrils filled with the scent of perfumes from countless women. The place was relatively dead this time of day. A half dozen lonely old men sat stationed at the bar, another handful were down in the lounge chairs closer to the action. The redhead I recognized from my last visit was performing to a heavy metal song, and using the pole like it was her own personal jungle gym.

Damn, that looks like a good workout.

Looking away from the action on stage, I sought out my

target. Eyes sweeping first left, then right, I cleared the space. But Finley was nowhere to be seen. Fine by me—I didn't particularly want her to know I was here on this recon mission at all.

I spotted the bald, grumpy-looking man that Finley had pointed out last time as her boss. He was wearing a different suit today, but it was just as gray and just as ill-fitting.

I approached him. "Great club. You the manager?"

He smiled crookedly, one gold tooth in the front glinting as it caught the strobe light above. "Thank you. Yes, I am. Can I help you with something?"

I shrugged like his answer wasn't important, but really, I wanted this information more than I wanted my next breath. I didn't know Finley's stage name, and didn't want to seem suspicious. But I figured that pretending to be an enthusiastic customer would be the best approach. This guy would be all too happy to see me come back and spend more money in his club. "I was hoping to see a dancer that I met here a couple weeks ago. Blonde, shoulder-length hair. Petite. About five-foot-five. I was wondering if I'd be able to see her here this weekend."

"Sounds like Stormy. She's getting pretty popular around here."

Stormy? The name certainly matched her mood. There had

to be a story there …

He grinned at me again, and I fought off the irrational urge to punch him. "She'll be here tonight, but she has Saturdays off."

"Thanks, man." I tipped my head at him and shoved my hands in my pockets.

"See ya 'round," he said as I retreated.

I sure as hell hope not. I'd be over the fucking moon if neither me nor Finley ever stepped foot into this dump ever again. Oh, excuse me, I meant *Stormy.*

Climbing back into my SUV, I made my plan. Saturday night. I would prove to her this could be a good thing. I had to.

***

West's Watering Hole was owned by my friend West, a tough-as-nails former SEAL. It was just the kind of casual place you came when you wanted a stiff drink and no one up in your business. It was popular amongst the local twenty-somethings for exactly that reason.

And tonight it was perfect. A not-too-rowdy Friday night crowd, and my two good friends Nolan and Lacey seated with me at a table in the corner. The huge diamond on her left finger was hard to miss. "Damn, girl. How do you walk around with that thing?" I asked.

Lacey laughed and fingered the large rock with an adoring look in her eyes. "He went a little overboard." She pretended to smirk at Nolan.

"I'd say. But I always knew you were the one." I smiled back at her.

"Even with that Daniella business?" she asked.

Nolan took her hand and gave it a squeeze.

His rocky past should have been a sore spot with his new fiancée. But it wasn't that way. Not with Lacey. She saw his faults and raised him, with a few of her own. Namely, hiding her identity from him when they first met. But neither had faults so deep that they couldn't be overcome. Hell, maybe unconsciously I was hoping for something similar to bloom between me and Finley. I'd never hid that fact I'd fucked up. I only wanted her to be able to see past it, see me for the man I was on the inside, just like Lacey had done with Nolan.

"We hardly see you anymore." Lacey set her elbows on the table and leaned in closer. "Do you have a girlfriend?"

Nolan snorted. "Doubt that, sweetheart."

I took a long sip of my beer and leaned in closer. "Actually, I do."

Their eyes widened. It was almost comical. They both

knew me well enough to know how un-fucking-likely that was.

"Well, tell us about her," Lacey encouraged before taking a sip from her straw.

"She's the best. Blond hair, big green eyes, sweet as can be...and she's one year old."

Lacey choked down her margarita. "W-what?"

Nolan's eyes narrowed on mine and I had a feeling he knew exactly where this was headed. What I couldn't read in his gaze was whether or not he would approve.

"Did Nolan ever tell you the story of our buddy Marcus?" I asked.

"Sutton," she supplied. "Yes, I remember."

I nodded, unsurprised. There wasn't much these two kept from each other, and besides, Nolan had gone and named his beloved bulldog after him. "Well, he was married. To a lady named Finley. Turns out she lives here in town, and I ran into her a couple months ago."

A crease formed in between Lacey's brows as she continued listening. Nolan's face was as impassive as ever. He rarely gave anything away. And Christ, I had no idea why I was spilling my guts now. Or why I hadn't told him earlier. Probably because of the look on his face. He swallowed, his throat working and mouth drawn into a tight line. I knew what I was doing was precarious. I was breaking the cardinal rule of the Man Code: don't get too close to your friends' women.

"And…" Lacey prompted.

I took another sip of my icy beer, hoping it would calm this fire raging inside me. "I started checking in on her. She has a daughter, Maple."

"Your new girlfriend." Lacey smiled.

"I was only joking, but yeah, Maple likes me a hell of a lot more than her pretty mama does."

Nolan was still quiet, his eyes dark and stormy.

"Aww…I'm sure you'll win her over," Lacey finished. "If you haven't noticed, you're quite a catch, Greyson Archer."

She might know the story of our fallen friend, but clearly she had no idea about the deep layers of remorse and guilt and animosity that had formed that only those of us close enough to the situation knew.

Lacey got up and excused herself to the bathroom.

Nolan cleared his throat, but stayed quiet. For several tense minutes.

Finally, the stony silence was too much for me. "Fucking say something, man."

He let out a deep sigh and knocked back his measure of whiskey in a single fiery gulp. "I don't know what you want me to say."

"Whatever it is you're thinking in that knotted-up brain of yours."

His jaw tensed, and he let out a breath. "This won't be tied up with a pretty bow at the end. She's not some woman you can just fuck and then forget."

"For fuck's sake. Don't you think I know that?" My heart rate started to accelerate and blood pounded in my ears. Who could forget a woman like Finley? Just the thought of anyone treating her that way...

"Then why don't you tell me what it is *you're* thinking? Because, honestly, I have no fucking clue what you're doing. A woman with a baby? That's not you, Grey. As long as I've known you, you've never even had a monogamous relationship. And now you're in deep with a single mom? And not just any single mom, but *Finley fucking Sutton*?"

I swallowed down my anger over his accusations and took a deep breath. I was getting pretty damn tired of people thinking I wasn't good enough that I'd fuck this up six ways from Sunday just like I had back then. But "I wasn't the same man I was back then. I played things much more cautious now. Nolan should know that. He should know I wouldn't get involved in something I couldn't see through to the end. I ignored the tiny doubting voice that whispered, *but what end will that be? What if, after all your best efforts, she still makes a decision you can't live with?*

I took a moment to compose myself. "On the surface, it's all wrong. I get that. But the truth is, Marcus is gone. And someone needs to watch out for Finley and the baby." Simple as that. It was in my eyes, anyway.

Nolan's eyes widened just slightly, betraying his surprise. "And you really think that man should be you? After everything that went down?"

I looked out into the distance, wishing for just a moment that I could be like every other carefree guy my age in this bar. Laughing at some stupid joke. Drinking with buddies. Chasing pussy. But I wasn't and I never would be. I'd seen too much, done too much, and now my brain filled with dark images when I closed my eyes at night. Even two years after escaping that world, its every moment still made my chest ache.

The only thing that chased away those bitter feelings was the time I spent with Maple and Finley. I felt something more burning inside me. The desire to be good enough for them. The desire to make up for all my terrible mistakes. I didn't want to be broken anymore. And I didn't want Finley to go on living a broken life, either. Especially when I'd had a hand in destroying her happily-ever-after in the first place.

"Never mind. I didn't expect you to understand. I only

listened to you whine and bitch about your fucked-up love life for, what, three months? You can fuck off, Nolan." I rose from the table and headed for the door before he could say another word.

Visiting Finley and Maple wasn't just about Marcus anymore. Maybe there had always been more. Whenever I stepped into their little family, I found more than just the motivation to become a better man. They helped me believe that, someday, I *could* be. And I'd be damned if I let that hope slip through my fingers.

***

It was nine o'clock on a Saturday night and I was totally out of my fucking element. A bottle of red wine tucked under one arm. A bouquet of wild flowers in the other. A condom tucked into my wallet, just in case. I was in foreign territory, and my entire body knew it – tense shoulders, my heart beating like a drum, and arousal barely contained beneath the surface.

Finley was standing at the doorway, watching me with a confused expression.

She looked gorgeous, makeup free, pink-painted toes, hair mussed and loose. Little cotton pajama shorts and a tank top that hugged her lush breasts.

"Maple's not here." She said the words, but she knew as well as I did I wasn't here for Maple.

"I know that." My voice was sure and confident.

"Then why are you ... oh." Finley shifted her weight, her eyes dropping from mine as she saw the wine and flowers. She could read it all, plain as day. I knew she could see my intentions, my uncertainty, and underneath it all, my desire. Maybe it was the desire to fix everything I'd broken, or maybe it was just my desire for her as a man desires a woman.

Normally when I felt that primal urge for sex, I headed to West's bar. I'd pick out a woman for the night. Share a few drinks with her, a few laughs. Later, we'd head back to my place and fuck until dawn. And that was it. I'd be set for a few months.

This ... with the courting and the nerves ... it was nothing like my standard operating procedure.

I'd never felt so stripped bare and vulnerable. Never put myself out there so completely with a woman before. But then again, Finley was unlike any woman I'd ever met.

And she was still just standing there. "Can I come inside?" I asked, heart in my throat.

She didn't say anything. But she opened the door wider.

With Nolan's words ringing in my ears, I stepped over the threshold, sure that whatever happened tonight had the power to heal us both.

Soon, my worries about coming here started to fade away. We sat together on the sofa, drinking wine and talking. Finley was in a somewhat deep and contemplative mood, if our discussion topics were any indication. We talked about life, goals she had for her future, for Maple's future.

Finley pulled her bare legs up onto the cushion beside me. "I want more for her than I had, you know. Broken home where I never had much of a relationship with my dad. I want her to go to college, meet someone nice, do whatever it is that makes her happy."

"You're a good mom. And a good person. I'm just ..." *A fuck-up.* I tried to ignore that nasty little voice in my head. As irritating as Nolan's lack of faith in me had been earlier, it was a lot harder to shut up my own self-hatred.

"Don't say it," Finley breathed.

That caught me off guard. A few short weeks ago, she would've been the first person in line to cut off my balls—in fact, she'd done it more than once. Now she wasn't even letting me mention my failures? Well, if she wanted to linger in this bubble where all the shit in our messy past didn't exist, that was fine by me. "I won't say it," I relented.

"There are some things I need to tell you."

She waited for me to continue, placing her hands in her lap.

"We were given a choice that day. We didn't have to go on that mission, yet I'd rallied for the chance to go into enemy territory, wanting to calibrate the telecommunications equipment I specialized in. If we could get some real intel, the entire mission would move forward and we'd all get to go home sooner."

She stayed quiet but her eyes were wide and filled with curiosity. I didn't know if I was telling her all this because I genuinely thought she needed to know, or if it was because I needed it off my chest. Scratch that--I knew exactly why I was telling her. I needed her forgiveness. Without it, I knew I could never forgive myself.

"Our commander was adamantly against it – said it was too dangerous. But I knew the risks and I was willing to take them. I also knew that Marcus, as one of my closest friends on the team, would insist on going with me."

Admitting it wasn't as scary as I thought it would be. Finley just blinked, quiet and contemplative. I always assumed this was her real issue-that I chose to do that mission despite not being required to go and knowing that Marcus would tag along.

"But I got the approval and we set off. It ended up being just the three of us – me, Marcus and Nolan. And then ..." God, I hated thinking about it, but it always found a way to replay in my brain. The scent of gunpowder burning my nostrils, the too-bright flash of heavy artillery fire momentarily blinding me. "And then he was hit. I saw the panic in his eyes. Already knowing it was too late, I rushed to administer first aid while Nolan held him. I muttered shit about his gorgeous wife and getting home in time to see the boxwood trees change. And while I held my breath with painstaking worry, he took his last."

She reached over and took my hand, giving it a firm squeeze.

"Are you okay?" I asked. I felt a little lighter with the words I'd bottled up for so long now out in the open between us.

"I'm okay," she said. "It's good to talk about it, I think. I've kept everything inside for so long that..." She stopped, and I squeezed her hand.

"I understand."

We sat in heavy silence for several moments, the mood changing all around us.

"Thank you for being so good with Maple."

"Of course." I stroked her cheek with my thumb. The look of longing in her eyes was unmistakable. She wanted this to be okay just as badly as I did.

I leaned in closer and she didn't pull away. Instead, she wet her bottom lip with her tongue. That was all the answer I needed. Cupping her jaw, I took her mouth in a hungry kiss. I'd waited all fucking week for this moment. And even though I'd told myself, as I pumped my cock each night, that her kisses couldn't possibly be as good as I remember...it was a damn lie. They were better. Her tongue matched mine stroke for stroke. Her pulse pumped against my thumb where I cradled her jaw, skimming along her neck. If one simple kiss could get me this worked up and ready, I was scared to see what would happen when we were skin to skin between the sheets.

Finley crawled closer toward me on the couch, our mouths breaking apart for just a second. But it was long enough for me to see her nipples were two firm points under her thin tank top and her eyes were dilated with desire. *For me.*

"Come here, sweetheart," I murmured, guiding her mouth back to mine, and praying to God this moment wasn't too good to be true.

Chapter Eight

Finley

I hadn't felt this good in more than two years. I'd convinced myself that I could shut off all my sexual feelings and just be a mom. But that was total bullshit, because right now, my entire skin was on fire. Feeling playful and a little tipsy, I decided to give Grey the lap dance he'd paid for all those weeks ago.

I swung my leg over to straddle him. Closing my eyes, I let him hold me, and kiss my mouth and neck. I moaned at the onslaught of sweet sensation. We were so close I could *feel* his answering groan, a primal sound of need that rumbled straight from his chest into me. His cock twitched between my thighs. So hot, so hard, so close to where I craved it.

He grabbed onto my hips and held me firmly against him. I could have continued our little game—scolded him, slapped his hands away, forced him to endure this erotic torture until I decided to relieve him. But right now, he wasn't a customer, and I wasn't a dancer. We were just a man and a woman. Two bodies that ached for each other. And when I opened my eyes, the roaring fire in his gaze made it impossible to wait any longer.

Kissing him hard, I ground into his erection. He growled and thrust up. Even separated by his jeans and my pajama shorts, the friction made me gasp. He shoved up my tank top and I moaned aloud as his mouth closed around my nipple. Tongue writhing, he suckled the sensitive bud until I squirmed, panting, dizzy. God, if he could melt me into a puddle just by playing with my breasts...how would that talented mouth feel on my clit? My pussy clenched at the thought.

He switched his mouth to my other breast, leaving the first nipple wet and aching to pebble in the cool air. His hands delved into my shorts, squeezing my ass, pulling me down harder against his firm bulge. My hips bucked shamelessly. His cock throbbed in response and I was dying to feel that throb from the inside. I wanted Grey to give me every indulgence I'd been denying myself for so long. All we had done was rub together through our clothes, but white heat was already building low in my belly, coiling tighter and tighter. Like we were a couple of horny teenagers necking in his backseat. I might have felt embarrassed if I weren't so damn desperate.

And then Grey's hands cupped even lower. I squeaked when his fingers brushed my outer pussy lips from behind. *Yes*, I wanted to cry, *touch me, please touch me, I don't even care how, just get me off, please.*

"Come on, baby," he panted. "Just let go. Let me make you feel good."

I moaned shamelessly into his mouth. But as the pleasure started its final climb, reality suddenly hit me. I was going to have a screaming orgasm on top of Greyson Archer. I was going to come my brains out barely ten feet from where my daughter slept at night, with the man who had taken her father away forever.

Guilt slammed into me. I struggled backwards onto my feet and yanked down my tank top, trying to ignore the crushing ache between my thighs. My whole body was crying out for me to get back down on that sofa and finish the job. But there was no way I could. Letting myself go in Grey's arms...it was all wrong.

"I'm sorry," I blurted before he could say anything. "No, I can't. I just can't."

Grey blinked up at me, the haze of lust not yet faded from his eyes. "You're throwing me out again?" He looked so bewildered and frustrated, and I couldn't blame him—I felt the exact same way.

"I'm sorry," I said again, uselessly.

"What is it you're after, Fin?" He stood up with a sigh. "All I want is to be there for you. I thought you wanted this...wanted me."

I swallowed hard and looked away. There had been no real anger in his tone, only confusion and concern. An honest affection that I suddenly wasn't sure I deserved.

He waited a few moments for my answer. Then, more somberly, he said, "There's nothing I can say to take your pain away, is there?"

I flinched.

"Is there?" he pressed.

Biting my lip hard, I finally replied, "No. There isn't." I forced myself to meet his gaze; he deserved at least that much. "It's never going to fade. It's never going to be okay. I'm always going to look at you and see..."

I didn't have to finish the sentence. Grey hung his head and cursed, his fists clenching at his sides. He wanted to fight me, to challenge me—but he knew I was right. Which only deepened my resolve.

"No matter our physical attraction, this will never work. It can't be. *We* can't." I choked the words out of my throat like sand, hoping I sounded confident and sure, when what I felt was shaky and weak.

Grey swallowed heavily, his throat working to hold back the argument I knew was on the tip of his tongue. I could read the man like a damn book. And this one didn't have a happy ending.

"So you need to leave," I went on. "Right now...and this time, don't come back."

His head snapped up. "But what about—?"

"I never should have let you see Maple in the first place. It'll only confuse her to have you popping in and out of her life all the time." Without giving him a chance to respond, I turned my back and opened the front door. The gesture was plain. *Get out.*

The night air rushed in to cool my face, flushed with shame and grief and the last stubborn traces of lust. For a moment, I squeezed my eyes shut against the tears that threatened. Grey walked past me and paused at the threshold. I kept my expression frozen as he looked at me for the last time, searching for a crack in my resolve, silently pleading for another chance.

His fingertips stoked my cheek – so light, so sweet – a soft gesture I didn't deserve after all the ways I'd probably tortured him. His eyes were so blue, so deep and so haunted, that I almost took back every nasty word I'd said. It was all right there on the tip of my tongue. But I knew I couldn't, wouldn't be able to live with myself if I did.

So all I said was, "Goodbye, Grey." And then I closed the door.

Chapter Nine

Greyson

The pain pounded through my head like a jackhammer through concrete.

"Fuck, make it stop," I groaned into my pillow. I pulled it over my head and squeezed my eyes shut, as if that could block out the noise. *That'll teach me to drink nothing but whiskey for three days straight...*

The pounding was so intense that, for a second, it transported me back to the war zone. Small-arms fire rattling, artillery shells screaming through the air, bombs detonating in the distance. Deafening and deadly.

I hated the memories that rushed in with that sound. As the team leader that day, I'd had to make a snap decision between several equally risky options. And while my choice did result in a casualty, it was impossible to say whether any of the other options would have fared any better. The scenario had no obvious right answer. And that was what kept me up at night. Replaying every move I'd made, trying to imagine every possible outcome, wondering if I could have saved him.

Cracking one eye open, my brain latched onto the fact it

was daylight out. Then the fog began to clear and I realized that wasn't my head pounding. It was my front door.

"Christ, hang on a second." I shoved the blankets back and tripped over my boots at the edge of the bed, stumbled my way out to the living room. Not an easy task when the floor was strewn with empty bottles, pizza boxes, and random articles of clothing.. Who the hell was at my door? It sounded like a goddamn elephant trying to charge through.

"What?" I pulled it open and saw a very pissed-off Nolan staring back at me.

"What the hell happened to you?" he barked.

I scrubbed a hand over my stubble-covered jaw. "Nothing." Nothing I wanted to talk about, anyway. Especially not with Nolan's judgmental ass.

"I was pounding on your door for fifteen minutes. Called your cell at least a dozen times."

I shrugged. "I was sleeping, you dick."

"It's ..." He glanced down at his wrist watch. "Twelve-fifteen. On a Monday."

Christ. It was Monday. I'd missed work. I took a deep, sobering breath and I knew things had to change. That final rejection by Finley had sent me into a tailspin. One I hadn't been able to pull myself out of all weekend long. I was fucking up at work because I was so distracted, consumed by thoughts of her.

And since my work was basically the only thing I had, our little cat-and-mouse game was finally done. Push me away, let me get close again, rinse and repeat. Kiss me like she wanted to ride my dick, then throw me out. I was done. Done bending over backwards and trying to make this work. But what stung even worse than losing a shot with Finley—what really killed me—was losing Maple in the process. They were a package deal. I mean, sure, I could try to maintain my relationship with her, but the way I felt right now, I didn't know if I had the balls to put myself in a position to get rejected and tossed out again.

Nolan stepped around me and headed inside. "Seriously, dude?" He shot me a questioning look.

I shrugged again, then sank down onto the couch.

"I'll make some coffee," he called from the kitchen. I heard him rattling around for a few seconds...and then I heard him talking on his phone. He was giving someone my address. "Yeah, today. And I'll pay you double."

I shook my head even though he couldn't see it. "What the hell are you doing?"

He entered the living room with two steaming mugs of coffee. "I hired a cleaning service. They'll be here in an hour."

"I have a cleaning lady who comes once a week."

"Yeah? And if she sees the place like this, she'll probably never come back. You went on a drunken bender. Trashed the place."

"It happens." After some of the shit we'd seen and done, he knew that as well as anyone.

He nodded. "It does. But this time, I'd like to know *why* it happened."

I shot him an icy glare. "I tried to open up to you once. At West's on Friday night. Remember how that discussion went? I don't care for an instant replay, do you?"

"Ah, fuck." He scrubbed a hand through his hair. "Maybe I overreacted, alright?"

I took a drink from my mug. "I'm listening."

Nolan rolled his eyes. "Just tell me what happened first."

"Well, turns out you were right all along. Shit got too real and she pushed me away, said she doesn't want to see me again."

"That's bullshit. I wasn't right." He let out a loud sigh through his nose. "On Friday...I was being a selfish prick. It felt weird to think about moving on from Marcus's memory. And that's what would happen if you took up with Finley. He'd be shoved to the backburner. I didn't like the idea of that. I didn't want anything about our lives to change—even though it was your and Finley's business, not mine. So I just steamrolled you instead of hashing things out like you needed. But after I cooled down and thought about it, I realized you were one hundred percent right. "

Slightly stunned by his naked honesty, I glanced up at Nolan, waiting for him to continue.

"A single woman on her own and a baby? They do need someone watching out for them. And there's no better man than you, Grey."

"Stop." I didn't need him blowing smoke up my ass.

"I mean it. You're the type of man who helps old ladies cross the street and pulls over to help when someone has a flat tire. Christ, you stopped our convoy in Baghdad to save a stray dog from wandering into the line of fire. You're a good fucking guy, Greyson."

I continued drinking my coffee, looking out into the backyard. None of it mattered. It didn't matter if my intentions were good. All Finley saw were my transgressions.

"There's no one who could be better for her and that baby than you. Marcus would have said so, too. I know it."

A lump formed in my throat. I wanted him to be right, I wanted this aching in my chest to ease up. But I had a feeling that wasn't going to happen anytime soon. "Doesn't matter." I stood up. "Didn't you hear what I said? She's done. That's it.

End of story."

But Nolan rose to his feet, too. "Since when are you a quitter?"

He was right. I was usually the one to volunteer for the riskiest, toughest assignments out there. I didn't believe in the word no. But this time, I was starting to realize...maybe I should.

Wait a minute. What was I thinking? Fuck that defeatist bullshit. The caveman in me wanted to take her by force if necessary – sit her down and make her listen to every reason I had about why this could work.

Chapter Ten

Finley

A scream of rage and fear dragged me awake.

Maple? I would recognize her little voice anywhere, but I'd almost never heard her howl like that. Had she fallen out of her crib somehow? Or did she just have a nightmare?

I struggled to push off the covers. But they were oddly heavy, so plush my hands sank into them. My limbs felt as weak and floppy as wet noodles. Had I picked up a bad flu? Great, that was all I fucking needed. No way could I afford to miss work.

But maybe I'd have no choice. My stomach rolled with nausea and even opening my eyes took effort. I blinked away a strange, swimming blur...then frowned. Something felt wrong here. This room was half the size of my entire apartment and way too clean. It had a high, peaked ceiling instead of flat stucco. Hardwood floors instead of stained carpet. Even the sheets against my skin felt weirdly smooth and cool.

Unless I was so sick I'd started hallucinating, I wasn't at home. So where the hell *was* I?

At the renewed wail from the next room, I forced myself

to sit up, ignoring the answering throb in my head. I could figure that out later. Wherever I'd gone, Maple had come with me, and she needed my help immediately. Without thinking, I jumped to my feet—only to be jerked up short. Frantically I glanced around and saw a thin silver chain dangling from a cuff on my wrist. It trailed onto the floor and under the bed, where the other cuff was locked around the bedpost.

What the actual fuck? My mouth dried up. Dizzy, I sat down again and tried to slow my pounding heart. My wobbly legs still wouldn't let me stand for too long; my arms weren't in much better shape. I wasn't strong enough yet to lift up the bed and slip the cuff off its leg. And I really didn't want to sit around waiting to recover. But maybe I could find something to break the chain or pick the lock?

I scanned the room, more slowly this time. The furniture was all matching cherry wood with fancy scrollwork: a nightstand, a chest-of-drawers, an armoire, and a vanity. I gasped at the sight of myself in the mirror. *Jesus, I look like shit.* My eye was surrounded by a huge, ugly purple bruise and my lip was swollen and bloodied. And was that a lump on my head? I fingered the spot gently and winced. Clearly I hadn't come to this place willingly. And if there'd been a fight, there must have been an attacker. A kidnapper...who might still be nearby. All the more reason to get my ass in gear.

I carefully stood back up and turned on the light. My chain was too short for me to reach most of the room—including the shuttered window—but I was able to start pawing through most of the furniture.

The chest-of-drawers contained panties and bras that I recognized as my own. *Lovely...a goddamn underwear thief.* Fortunately, I had woken up in my clothes, so I didn't have to deal with the mental image of my kidnapper undressing me while I was unconscious.

The armoire stood open to reveal a single yellow sundress. It wasn't mine, and I tried not to think too hard about the fact that it seemed my size. *If he expects me to wear that, he can fucking choke on it.*

As I searched the room, my memories of last night came trickling back. I'd managed to kick Grey out of our life, but not out of my mind. Conflicted and miserable, with a massive amount of pent-up sexual frustration, I had slogged through my dance routines, just trying to survive until the end of the evening. And the customers could tell I was phoning it in. At least, one customer could.

Brant had come up to the stage to ask me what was wrong. Normally I'd remind him to buy a lap dance if he wanted one-on-one time, but I didn't have the emotional energy to handle him gracefully. So I had let Bruce tell him off and show him back to his table. But Brant couldn't seem to keep his ass in his seat. He kept walking up, over and over, as if he didn't notice me ignoring him. When he'd reached out to rest his hand on my ankle, Bruce had tossed him out into the parking lot.

But he still couldn't take the hint. After my shift finally ended, I'd trudged out to my car, only to almost run face-first into Brant.

"Let me help you, Finley," he had pleaded. "I just want to be there for you."

Rubbing my forehead, I'd squinted at him through the sickly glow of the sodium lamps. "Have you been standing out here all night?"

"Of course. That's what you do when you love someone."

That was when I'd snapped. Everything hurt so bad—my feet, my back, my heart—and I just couldn't take anymore. Night after night, I'd gritted my teeth and smiled through Brant's bullshit. I'd shaken my ass in high heels when I was so tired I could barely think straight. I'd worked entire nights without even earning my house fee. I'd eaten thousands of ramen cups and PB&J sandwiches. I'd paid my bills in wadded-up singles while the bank tellers whispered and pointed at me. I'd chased Grey away forever. I'd been such a good girl for so long, and what did I have to show for it? Where had it gotten me? Trapped in a parking lot at two in the morning with a delusional moron. His big tips couldn't buy another second of my patience.

Staring Brant square in the eye, I'd snapped, "What the hell are you talking about? You don't love me. You don't even know me. And I sure as hell don't love you."

He'd blinked several times in quick succession, as if I'd suddenly sprouted a second head. "But...I don't understand," he'd squeaked. "What do you mean? I've always thought you were so perfect, and you're always so nice to me..."

"That's called customer service, Brant. Do you think the girl who makes your coffee wants your dick, too?" With that, I turned on my heel and left him.

Brant had just watched, stunned, as I got into my car and drove away. I didn't give a fuck. All I could think about was food, sleep...and Grey. I'd been so distracted, it was a miracle I hadn't gotten in a car wreck. I'd walked to my door and was flipping through my keys. Then a figure in the darkness, hands digging into me, a sickly sweet smell, thrashing and kicking and biting and suddenly falling, falling...

I froze, my hands buried in a mound of spare linens. *Brant.* Suddenly everything clicked. He must have followed me home and chloroformed me. He'd made no secret of being obsessed with me...but I had never dreamed he'd take it this far. I bit my lip, holding back a wave of tears and nausea.

Despite how close I felt to a nervous breakdown, I gave a very quiet cheer when I found my purse in the very back of the vanity's bottom drawer. I'd just assumed that Brant would confiscate all my stuff. He was either incredibly confident or incredibly stupid. I eagerly dumped out my purse on the bed and clawed through the pile. This nightmare would all be over as soon as I found my phone.

Two minutes later, my heart had sunk back into my roiling stomach. Brant *had* thought of taking everything vital. My phone, wallet, and keys were gone. There was only one thing I could put to any use: Grey's business card. I'd shoved it into the hidden zippered pocket of my purse, crumpling and dirtying the cardstock, unknowingly saving it from Brant's attention. I didn't even know why I'd kept it at all, at that time Grey was the last person I wanted to call.

But now he was the first person I wanted to call. If I called the police, Brant could shoot first and ask questions later—leaving me alone again, this time with a pissed-off madman. He'd already managed to overpower me once, so who knew what he was capable of? No, I needed someone with stealth as well as strength. Someone who could get in, get the job done, and get out before Brant even knew we were missing.

I memorized the contact number on the card and tucked it away again. There had to be a phone somewhere in this godforsaken house.

Just as I'd stashed my purse back in the drawer, the doorknob turned. My heart jumped into my throat. I quickly sat back on the bed and tried to look innocent.

The door cracked and Brant's beady eye peeked through. At the sight of me, he smiled and let himself in. "I see someone's awake," he said. His tone was gently teasing, as if he'd found me sleeping late on a Sunday morning.

"Where am I?" I asked, trying not to let my voice tremble.

His cheerful expression didn't slip an inch. "Your new home."

I repressed a scowl. *Like fucking hell it is.*

He strolled past me and over to the window, where he opened the blinds to reveal a fiery sunset. "My family always loved to spend summers in the mountains. They really are the best vacation spot. No WiFi signal, no phone reception, just good old-fashioned quality time."

I screamed internally. *Mountains?* The nearest ranges were four hours to the east and twice as long to the west. I must have been knocked out for longer than I'd thought. More importantly, even if I managed to find my phone or steal his, it would be useless here. And he'd probably pay extra attention to the rooms with landlines. If there even were any.

Brant was still gazing out the window, admiring the vivid desert sunset. What the hell was wrong with him? His *everything is totally normal* act was unbelievably creepy. My heart was still pounding and the desire to get to my daughter burned like a wildfire inside me. But I had to play nice for a minute and try to get some information from this psycho.

But what leapt out of my mouth was, "Why are you doing this?"

He turned his head, looking mildly surprised. "I just want to make my two girls happy."

"So you kidnapped us?" I asked before I could stop myself.

He sighed. "All I want is for you to give me a chance, Finley. Let me show you I'm worthy of your love." He crossed the room again and sat down beside me on the bed. I flinched. "I know you'll learn to enjoy life here."

Half of me was imagining clawing his eyes out or strangling him with my chain. But the other half was frozen in terror. If my attack failed to knock him out, it would just anger him...and he might hurt Maple or separate us as punishment. I had to play along with his twisted little game. Just long enough to get Maple back in my arms, figure out where the hell he'd taken me, and steal ten minutes with a phone. In that order. If I earned his trust, he'd slip up sooner or later. I swallowed down my anger.

"I'll...I'll try," I choked out.

His face lit up. "Great! We can—"

"But I need to see Maple first," I interrupted. Her cries had gradually petered out, but that was even more worrisome than her screaming her head off.

"Who?" He looked towards the door. "Oh, her. Of course. Let me get you out of here."

As he took a tiny key from his pocket, his arm brushed aside his suit jacket. I swallowed hard at the glimpse of black metal. A handgun. He had a fucking gun tucked into his waistband. I didn't think I could get any more scared, but hot fear like I'd never felt before raced through me.

Showing no sign of noticing my panic, Brant unlocked my wrist cuff. Then he led me down the hall to another small bedroom. Its rose-pink walls were scarred with tape-marks from old posters. The furniture had been shoved aside to make room for a crib with chipped white paint—clearly a relic that had been dug out of storage.

My stomach unknotted with sheer relief when I saw Maple fast asleep. Poor thing...she must have exhausted herself crying. I rushed close, only to wrinkle my nose. It smelled like her diaper had been full for hours. I ground my teeth. How could this idiot not know the first thing about kids? Didn't he say he had a family?

Maple's eyes fluttered open when I picked her up. She blinked, confused for a second, then smiled at me. "Mommy," she cooed.

"Yes, honey." I swallowed back sudden tears. "Mommy's here."

Satisfied with that, she popped her thumb back into her mouth. *Thank God she's okay.* I glanced around and saw Brant standing in the doorway. "Do you have a changing table?"

"Oh..." He looked lost. "Just use the bed for now."

My diaper bag sat on the twin bed. Even if he didn't know much about babies, he'd at least thought to grab that.

After I finished changing Maple, making no effort to avoid dirtying the crisp white linen, Brant motioned to me. "Come on, let me give you the grand tour."

Keeping Maple locked in my arms—there was no fucking way I was ever letting her out of my sight again—I followed him upstairs.

I kept a smile frozen on my face as he showed me around my prison. Not only to keep the psycho placated, but to keep Maple at ease, too. I had to show her that Mommy was okay. I just wished it were true.

Upstairs, photos hung on every wall, showing Brant, a short blonde woman, and an aloof-looking teenaged girl. There was a definite family resemblance. But this house had too many empty rooms. The closets only held men's clothes and shoes. One cluttered nightstand in the master bedroom, the other one bare. The place was so neat, so lifeless, that it would have felt like a hotel if everything weren't covered in a layer of dust.

What the hell was going on? Didn't Brant always wear a wedding ring whenever he came to pester me? The small bedroom where I'd found Maple must have once been his daughter's room. I realized I wasn't the only person here who was clinging to something long gone.

Well, boo fucking hoo for him. Even in the worst depths of my grief, I'd somehow managed not to run around kidnapping people. Something must have been twisted inside Brant from the very beginning; whatever had happened to his family had just brought it to the surface.

With a shudder, I realized something else. The woman in all the family photos looked a lot like me. Or rather, I looked like her. Green eyes, long face, and blonde, slightly wavy hair.

I guess I know why he chose me now. Gee, what an honor.

Chapter Eleven

Greyson

Life had pretty much returned to normal. My house was now in order, and I was back to work. But the feeling of being punched in the gut still lingered. The sleepless nights. The breathlessness. The constant body aches. No matter what I tried, it was always there—this haunting feeling in my chest, weighing me down. I worked overtime, trained extra hard at the gym, and fought to get my head back on straight. Nolan had been absolutely right. Either that, or my male pride just got the best of me. Even if Finley and I weren't meant to be, I needed to talk to her once more and make sure there were no hard feelings. If I was lucky, maybe we'd even discuss how I could keep Maple in my life.

After work, I decided I'd drive over to the club. It was more neutral territory than her apartment. I could say what I needed to say and leave on my terms. She couldn't bar me from the door or throw me out.

When I got there, that sleazy manager in his baggy suit was lingering near the bar, flirting with one of the cocktail waitresses. I strode toward him as anger built inside me. I would always hate that these men got to see Finley's bare skin and curves...while I never would again.

I took a deep breath and stopped beside him.

"Can I help you?" he asked, clearly annoyed that I'd interrupted them long enough for the waitress to scurry away.

"I'm here to see Stormy."

He squinted at me. "I remember you." Then he shook his head. "I'm sorry to tell ya, buddy, but Stormy's gone."

I blinked. I'd been prepared for her avoiding me, but this was ridiculous. "What do you mean, *gone?*"

"She skipped out on her shift yesterday. Hasn't shown up for today's, either." He looked down at his watch and frowned. "This isn't the type of job people put in a two weeks notice and want references for...when girls are done, they just split. That's it." He shrugged. "Sorry, man."

Fuck. A sinking feeling formed in my gut and I took a step back.

"Layla's nice. She'll take good care of you." He tipped his chin toward a girl who was approaching from the left. It was the redhead I remembered from the first time I was here.

"Hi, handsome. Want some company?" she asked, her voice lifting in a sweet Southern accent. That was exactly what she'd said back then, too. *Guess she's got a routine worked out.*

"Yeah, sure." I took her hand and led her over toward the lounge area, where I hoped it would be quieter. We sank down into the plush chairs, and just as I had hoped, the thumping music from the DJ's set wasn't quite so loud back here.

Layla leaned closer. "So, what would you like, darling? A lap dance to start?"

I pulled my wallet from my back pocket and peeled off a couple of twenties from the stack. "Did you know Stormy?"

Her eyes lifted from the bills I was holding and narrowed on mine. "Yeah, I knew her." Her tone was laden with suspicion.

"Well, Finley," I clarified, "she was my friend. I knew her husband, fought alongside him in the Middle East."

Understanding flashed in her brown eyes and she nodded somberly. "You're Greyson."

I nodded.

"Hold on. There's someone you need to talk to." She rose to her feet, only a little shaky in her high heels, and scurried away into the darkness.

What the fuck was going on here?

***

An hour later, I had gone through Finley's apartment in meticulous detail, being sure not to miss even the smallest of clues. I could have tried to talk the landlord into opening the door for me, but I was a damn fine lock-pick and it'd be a shame to waste all that training.

The club's house mom, Ginger, had told me about a customer named Brant who seemed to be fixated on Finley. Her friend Layla backed up that story, sharing an ominous encounter from a couple weeks ago where he'd waited for her in the parking lot. I remembered driving up right after that, and how Finley had tried just a little too hard to seem unruffled. I didn't want to jump to conclusions, but the facts were that nobody had heard from her in days, and my soldier's instincts smelled trouble. And I wasn't the only one; Ginger seemed to think Finley hadn't just quit – that there was foul play at work. I tried to come up with an innocent explanation. Maybe she'd cut and run after things between us went south. Maybe she'd headed to Florida for a visit with Marcus' parents. But nothing added up.

And when I got to her place and saw her car there, but she wasn't – I knew it was something bad. Her place was picked over, and it looked like someone had packed quickly. I'd been in enough hostile situations to recognize one, and while nothing really looked out of place here, all my hunches were up. The only things missing were her undergarments and some of Maple's clothes. Their dresser drawers were left open and messy.

I sat down on the end of her mattress. I'd never been inside her bedroom before, and it was pretty bare-bones. One twin-sized bed and a narrow dresser, making me think she'd sold off her marital bed and furniture. A framed photo of Marcus stood on her nightstand. I picked it up and looked down at the half-lidded eyes of my friend as he smiled back at me. If she really had split town, she never would have left this behind.

"I'm going to find her, buddy," I promised.

After locking up behind me, I dialed my boss, Jerry Barton.

"I'm listening," he answered on the first ring.

"We've got a situation, Jerry. I need you to dig up everything on a guy named Brant Rockwell. He lives in the area. Works as an accountant, I believe. Frequents the Dolly House Gentleman's Club."

"What's going on?" he asked. I knew he was already taking down my every word.

"A new case I'm requesting. Finley's missing and I have good intel that that asshole was obsessed with her. He clearly has something to do with her disappearance. I've got to make this right."

Jerry paused, then cleared his throat. "I'm sorry, there's no delicate way to say this...but Nolan mentioned something that day you didn't show up to work. Are you sure she isn't just avoiding you?"

"Jerry, with all due respect, I know the difference between

a break-up and a fucking kidnapping. No one's seen or heard from her in two days. Her car is parked in the lot and she's gone."

"I had to ask," he said, his tone softer.

"I get it. But I'm going after her."

"Fine. I'll give you and Nolan clearance for whatever resources you need. Bring our girl home."

"Nolan's not involved. I'm going alone." Climbing in my SUV, I gunned the engine, heading toward home to prepare for war if need be.

"Cut the crap, Greyson. So you and Nolan had an argument—get over it. Or take someone else, if you want. Sean and Davis are free today."

"That's not the reason. Nolan and I are square. But this is for me to set right. No one else." I failed Marcus that day, and while nothing will ever make up for that fact, it had to be me.

"I can't advocate that, Greyson. You know the risks of flying solo. No lookout or driver or gunner, no backup to call on if shit hits the fan..."

"I know. But I need to do this." I ended the call and stepped on the gas. Every second counted if Finley and Maple were in danger.

Chapter Twelve

Finley

Soon after sunrise on the third day, I carried Maple upstairs and set her in her high chair. Brant was already sitting at the kitchen table, with his laptop open in front of him and a cup of black coffee by his elbow. He looked up and smiled at the sound of my footsteps. "Good morning, sunshine. What's for breakfast?"

Whatever you're making, asshole, was what I wanted to snap. Which decade were we living in again? He'd clearly been up for a while, but he hadn't lifted a finger to put food on the table. If only I could starve him to death by pretending to be a bad cook.

"Morning," I replied tonelessly. "I was thinking pancakes."

Ever since the first day, I'd struggled to maintain the fragile balance between making him angry and coming across as flirtatious. I had to keep things strictly civil. If he thought I'd warmed up to him too much...

I still slept in the downstairs guest room where I'd first woken up. Unchained now, so I could use the bathroom and reach Maple if she cried. Brant hadn't made me spend the night in his bed yet. Although he had broached the subject—and I'd tried not to shudder too visibly—he hadn't pushed it. But I was sure it was only a matter of time. And when that time came, I didn't know what I'd do.

Brant beamed and turned to Maple. "Ooh, pancakes. How would you like that, darling? With lots of maple syrup for my maple girl?"

She just gave him a slow, big-eyed blink. *Your girl?* she seemed to say. *Who the hell are you and why are you talking to me?* I chuckled to myself. She might not have been old enough to understand the details, but she could sense when things weren't quite right.

I eyed Brant's laptop as I cut open a bag of pancake mix and dumped it into a bowl. A red Ethernet cable looped from his computer to a jack on the wall under the table. Signal or no signal, he needed to keep up with work, and for that he needed Internet. But he hadn't given me a moment alone with any of his electronics.

While pouring the batter onto the griddle, I commented as casually as I could manage, "By the way, we're out of diapers." I had been changing Maple almost every hour to use them up as fast as possible. Brant had only packed a small stash. I figured he only had two options here: He would bring us back to civilization in order to keep an eye on us, giving me the chance to make a scene, find a phone, maybe even just run for it. Or he'd leave us behind, letting me explore the house unsupervised.

Your move, you twisted son of a bitch.

"Oh, dear. I guess I'll have to drive downtown today."

I let myself grin, knowing he couldn't see it when I faced the stove. "Can we come along with you? I want to see if I can find Maple's usual toddler snacks. She can be picky."

He frowned. "I don't think that's a good idea. Your eye's still black and blue...we don't want to attract attention. People are probably looking for you."

Privately, I doubted that. I had no family living nearby, no real friends. The other strip club employees would be the only people wondering about me, but strippers unexpectedly quit their jobs all the time. They'd probably just grumble about having to pick up my shift. But what I said was, "You're right. It would look suspicious." I started to flip the gently bubbling pancakes.

Brant shut his laptop and looked at Maple again. "Maybe this would be a good chance for some father-daughter time."

I froze, almost dropping a pancake on the floor. That idea hadn't occurred to me. Just the thought of leaving her alone with him was too horrifying for words. And if he separated us, I'd be stuck waiting until they got back to grab Maple and escape. I had to shut down his idea fast. But my mind was paralyzed. *Quick, Finley, come up with a reason...* My insides felt like they were being twisted with a fork.

"She only lets me pick her up," I blurted. That was only a partial lie. Before Greyson barged into our lives, Maple had been a one-hundred-percent mommy's girl. "She'll start screaming and carrying on in the store."

"Is that so?" I held my breath as Brant looked at her. Finally, he sighed. "Too bad. I guess it'll have to wait until we know each other better."

I rushed our heaping plates to the table. The pancakes tasted like sand and rasped down my throat like concrete. Mechanically, I forced myself to keep chewing and swallowing, my heart pounding in anticipation. In contrast, Brant ate with such leisure that I thought I might scream. He poured himself a second cup of coffee and I briefly, vividly fantasized about stabbing him with my fork. *Finish your goddamn breakfast and get in the car, already!*

At long last, the front door closed. Maple and I were alone for the first time in three days. The bad news was that Brant had taken his laptop and cell with him. On some level, though, I'd expected that. What mattered was how long my window of opportunity was. Without knowing where we were—and therefore where the nearest town was—I could only guess when he'd get back. But an hour seemed like a safe minimum.

Taking Maple's hand, I started searching the house for a landline phone. But the longer I explored, the lower my heart sank. All I found were bare jacks. Brant had pulled the phones themselves out of the walls and either hidden or destroyed them. I checked the clock. Shit, I only had twenty minutes before I had to start watching my back. That wasn't enough time to turn the house upside-down looking for phones that might not even exist anymore. I sat down on the cold hardwood floor, head on my knees, crushed.

Then tiny fingers touched my hair. I looked up into Maple's wide jade eyes, full of worry. "Mommy?" she asked softly.

I sniffed back the tears that threatened. I had to keep it together for my daughter's sake. But what the hell was I going to do now? Just walk out into the wilderness and hope I could flag down a passing car? I still didn't have the slightest clue where we were. And Brant probably wouldn't have left us here alone if there was any help within walking distance.

But there was nothing else left to try. *It's worth a shot...*

I stood and scooped Maple up against my chest. She made an uncertain noise. But her small hands held tight around my neck, as if she knew how serious this was. I hoped she didn't understand too much; this nightmare could cost her years of therapy later in life.

"It's okay, sugar pie," I murmured as confidently as I could. "We're just going for a walk." *The longest walk of our lives.* I hurried downstairs to the front door, anxious to make the most of our head start.

Just as I touched the doorknob, my heart stopped at the crunch of gravel in the driveway. How could he be back already? I squinted through the frosted glass. That car didn't look like Brant's sedan. It was too big, wrong color, wrong style...

My heart bounded back to life. Could it be? Was I dreaming? A tall figure got out and loped up the driveway.

"Ay-son!" Maple squealed.

I gasped and fumbled with the lock. It *wasn't* too good to be true. I wasn't going to wake up in that bed yet again, sick with dread, fresh despair twisting in my gut. Greyson really was here. He had come for me and he would make everything okay again, just like he did before. In that moment, the image of us sitting at my crappy little table eating mac 'n cheese ached just as sharply as my memories of Marcus.

I flung open the door and Grey was standing there on the porch, so perfect, my savior. His handsome features were set in a look of pure determination. It was a good thing Brant had gone out, because Grey probably would have killed him on the spot.

Relief shone in his eyes like dawn. "Finley, thank God. Is he here?"

I quickly shook my head. "No, but he'll be back soon," I

managed to croak.

Maple struggled in my arms, giggling. I put her down and she grabbed Grey's leg like a fireman's pole. He ruffled her golden hair. "That's okay. I wasn't planning on hanging around."

He followed me downstairs and helped me throw all of our meager belongings into a trash bag. As we finished, I turned to see him holding Maple in the crook of one muscled arm. Something about seeing him like that—a strong protector carrying my baby—cracked my heart wide open. All the stress and fear of the past three days finally hit me. I buried my face in my hands and started sobbing. I didn't need to stay stoic anymore. If only for a moment, I could let go. I could let my tears wash me clean.

Firm warmth closed all around me. Grey's other arm, with Maple pressed between us. "What's wrong?" he asked. His voice rumbled beneath my cheek. "Are you hurt?"

Swallowing hard, I gave him a weak smile. "It's okay," I said, and meant it this time.

Grey may not have understood why I was crying, but he kept on holding me. Maple did her part by reaching up to pet my chin.

A minute later I stepped back, sniffed loudly, and said, "Let's hurry."

He nodded and started back upstairs, still carrying Maple. I followed with the trash bag.

Once we were all safely in the car, Grey pulled out his phone and dialed a number I didn't recognize. "Mr. Barton," he said, with no preliminaries. "I've secured the hostages. The target should arrive within the hour. I'd like to have a little party waiting for him when he gets back...arrest him for kidnapping and assault."

Grey paused for a moment to listen, then turned to me and asked me in an undertone, "Was he armed?"

I nodded. "He kept a pistol tucked into his waistband."

"Tell the state troopers he's armed and dangerous," Grey said. Then he hung up and gunned the engine. With a spray of gravel, we started bumping down the mountainside, heading on our long way home.

Chapter Thirteen

Greyson

With hot blood still raging through my veins, it took everything I had just to keep driving east. I wanted to go back there and wait for Brant to return. To make him feel the same agony I'd felt for the last three days searching for Finley and Maple—let alone the pain and fear he'd put *them* through. But getting them home as soon as possible was more important than revenge. Knowing they were both safe, and next to me, I kept driving, putting as much distance as possible between them and danger's path.

Finley sobbed quietly in the passenger's seat, her hands shaking in her lap, while Maple napped behind us in her car seat, unaware of everything that had gone on. Or maybe, somehow her little mind had absorbed some of it and the stress had exhausted her.

I curled my fists around the steering wheel and settled in. We had a long drive ahead of us and there was no way in hell I was ready to take Finley back to her apartment. Honestly, I had no intention of letting her out of my sight again, but I didn't know how she was going to take that. So I just drove.

A couple hours later, Maple was restless and we were all hungry. I navigated to an acceptably nice hotel off the interstate and pulled the SUV to a stop.

"What are we doing here?" Finley asked. There was smudged makeup under her eyes and she looked exhausted. I couldn't even imagine what she had been through. We would get to that, but first I needed them settled.

"We'll rest. Let Maple run around and play. Order room service. Come on." I turned off the car and got out.

Finley gave a soft sigh, but didn't argue. We checked into a room with two double beds and requested a crib be brought up. I ordered a feast from room service while Finley changed Maple's diaper and unpacked what little luggage she had.

"Are we really staying the night here? We're only a few hours from home," she asked after I hung up the phone.

"It's the safest thing to do for now. Brant knows where you live." *Obviously.* "Until I hear that he's in custody, I can't have you going back to your apartment and have him try to come after you again."

I checked my phone again. No word from Jerry yet. The idea of that guy being hauled off in handcuffs—preferably with a little police brutality—was the only thing that could ease my mind right now. Until I knew for sure, we'd lay low.

"Once we eat, we'll find a store and pick up some supplies."

We'd gotten out of there so fast, all they had were the clothes on their backs and a few meager articles thrown in a trash bag.

Finley sunk down onto the bed and nodded. "I just feel like an epic failure. I put my daughter in jeopardy. Probably scarred her for life."

"Don't say that. She's fine. Look at her."

Maple was toddling around the room while babbling into the TV remote, pretending it was a phone.

Finley wiped a tear from her cheek with the back of her hand. "How can she be *fine*? We were kidnapped, Grey. By some psychopath from a job I should have never even ..."

"Hey." I put my hand on her shoulder. "You were doing what you had to do to make ends meet."

"That's it. That's all you're going to say? No, *I told you so*?" There was so much pain in her eyes. It sliced straight through me and made my heart stutter.

I shook my head. That would be an asshole of a thing to say at a time like this. Now, if she tried to continue working there, then all bets were off.

"How did you know something was wrong? How did you know to come find me?" she asked.

"I just knew." *Because you're mine to protect now.*

Her eyes grew wider and I thought maybe, just maybe, she was starting to understand that.

When our food arrived, we ate in front of the TV, watching some kid's show that kept Maple occupied. Afterwards, we just kept moving as if on auto-pilot, putting on our shoes and piling into the car. I wanted nothing more than to pull Finley into the bed with me, wrap my arms around them and just hold her. Let her calm down like I knew she needed to. But we had responsibilities first. We had a baby with a very soggy diaper, and in a couple hours, it would be bedtime. I wanted to make sure her routine stayed as normal as possible. So we headed into town to a super-store and pushed a shopping cart through the aisles, tossing essentials in as we went. Lavender baby shampoo, diapers, snacks, and a pair of yoga pants for Finley. She grumbled something about *that fuckstick only packing her lingerie and dresses.* I clenched my jaw and kept my mouth shut.

A little while later, back at the hotel, Finley gave Maple a bath and then I diapered and dressed her in her new fuzzy pajamas while Finley showered herself. It was the first time I'd ever changed a diaper, but rather than it being gross, I felt proud taking care of her.

Finley took her time in the shower, and that was fine with me. I figured she had some things to work through. By the time

I heard the shower turn off, Maple was sound asleep in her temporary crib.

The bathroom door opened with a rush of warm steam. Finley was dressed in her new yoga pants and an oversized t-shirt, and her damp hair hung in loose, golden waves around her shoulders. With her skin scrubbed clean of makeup and her pink cheeks glowing from the warm shower, she looked years younger. Softer, somehow. But those brilliant green eyes still sliced right through me.

The desire to touch her and kiss her rose inside me. But my feelings went beyond the physical—further than I'd ever thought possible. Her matter-of-fact strength left me awestruck. She had endured so much for so long. I'd seen more blood and death and pain than any man should, and it had gouged dark trenches into my soul. But all of life's ugliness had barely scratched hers. And what few imperfections she had only made her more beautiful. Her scars spoke quietly, yet undeniably: *I survived. I outlasted the enemy. And then I moved on to the next day's battle.* How many soldiers could go on fighting with no end in sight, no glory or backup or even the promise of victory?

Suddenly it hit me. Something that had been staring me in the face for a long time. Standing there in that crappy hotel room, gaping at Finley like an idiot, both of us still trembling with leftover adrenaline...I realized just how deeply I'd fallen in love with her.

Fuck, I was in so much trouble. And I didn't even care.

"Wow. She's out?" Finley asked, crossing the room over to the empty bed across from the one I was sitting on.

I nodded. "She went down without a peep."

"She's one resilient kid."

"A lot like her mom in that regard."

She made a noise of disagreement.

"I've got some more good news. Barton called and confirmed that Brant is in custody. He was arrested and charged with aggravated kidnapping, assault, endangering a child, carrying a weapon without a permit, and a whole bunch of other things. He'll be facing serious time."

"Thank you." Her hands trembled in her lap.

I nodded. "You'll have to make a statement to the police when we get back into town."

"That's no problem."

After what Brant had done, she'd have no problem making sure that he got the maximum punishment coming to him. I took a deep breath, steadying myself. There was so much more I wanted to ask her, things we needed to talk about, but I wouldn't push her tonight. She was obviously tired and exhausted. Her eyes looked heavy and her breathing was shallow. She was laying on her side on the bed, watching me, and I mirrored her pose, laying across from her. The desire to touch her creamy skin, to kiss her mouth, to make sure every last inch of her was okay would have to wait.

"I need to know ... did he touch you?" I asked.

She shook her head. "No. Thank God. He didn't try anything like that. But if you hadn't gotten there ..."

I nodded, utterly fucking relieved. I was sure that Brant would have tried something eventually. And just like he'd taken her against her will, the word *no* wouldn't have mattered to him.

Finley pulled the covers around her and I flicked off the lamp. "Get some sleep," I said. "We'll figure everything out in the morning." *I hope.*

***

After a pancake breakfast at a diner along the highway, we were finally back in town. I pulled into Finley's apartment complex and took a moment to compose myself. I didn't want this to end in a fight, but I had a feeling it might, and I was prepared to go to battle.

Once inside, we watched Maple run straight to her stuffed owl and squeal with delight. Finley's eyes found mine and she smiled—for the first time since this whole ordeal began, I was willing to bet.

"It's good to be home, isn't it, baby?" Finley said.

If she thought this was home, she was kidding herself. "Get packed up, I'll wait." I crossed my arms over my chest.

Her smile vanished, eyes narrowing. "Wait. What?"

"If you think after everything that's happened, I'm letting you guys stay here ..." I shook my head, my stiff posture matching hers.

"And here I thought you were being so sweet and helpful." She planted her hands on her hips. "But once again, you're just trying to control the situation. How many times do I have to tell you I can fend for myself? Plus, Brant's locked up. You said we don't have to worry about him anymore."

I growled out a curse under my breath. Her constant rejection didn't just hurt, it fucking *stung*. I'd been pushed too far and I was ready to snap. With Maple playing across the room, I leaned in close to Finley; I didn't want her daughter to hear the ugly venom in my voice. "I'm done. You pushed too far this time. I don't give a flying fuck what you want anymore. Do you know what I went through knowing you two were in danger? And it's become pretty damn obvious that this place isn't safe. So I'm not asking you again. I'm telling you. Pack your shit.

Please. We're leaving in fifteen minutes."

We squared off, gazes locked together, neither of us willing to budge. But this was it. If she pushed me again, I might just walk out of her life for good. This moment meant everything.

Just as Finley angrily opened her mouth, a knock sounded at her door.

Her brow crinkled in confusion, she growled and whipped around to open up. It was a thin, jowly man with a bad comb-over and a handful of wrinkled papers. Based on the pieces of their hushed conversation I strung together, he was her landlord, and she was late on her rent. Very late—more than what she would've missed while being held prisoner.

Watching this train wreck of a conversation almost made me feel bad for Finley. None of this was her fault, and her dignity had already taken a beating lately. But it was time for her to realize that she wasn't in this life alone. She didn't have to prove anything. She didn't have to shoulder every burden like it was her own personal cross to bear. I wanted to help. I was here for her, and I always would be. Time and time again, I'd demonstrated that she could rely on me, and still she was fighting her way through life alone, one awful situation after another.

"I told you one more time and I'd evict you," the landlord said, his voice stiff. Clearly this wasn't his favorite part of the job.

Adding this complication to an already volatile situation was like throwing gasoline on a fire. Finley straightened her shoulders and gritted her teeth. "Fine. Then consider us evicted. Bye." She slammed the door in his face and stalked into the bedroom, me on her heels and Maple toddling along behind us.

I watched as Finley grabbed a duffel bag from her closet and started stuffing the clothes from her dresser inside. She looked up at me and I expected some smart quip about me getting what I wanted. Instead, her eyes were simply sad.

"Will you go pack up that bureau?" She tipped her chin to the tall dresser in the corner of her bedroom. "It's Marcus's stuff and I can't bear to go through it right now."

"Of course."

While I packed up a few framed photos, dog tags, a folded flag and a box of old letters, Finley threw clothes and shoes and toys into a couple of bags.

"What about the furniture?" I asked when she looked like she was through.

"Maple will need a crib...but the rest..." She shrugged.

"We'll get her a new one."

Finley breathed deeply for the first time since we arrived. "Let the property management deal with it. It was all secondhand anyhow."

I lifted Maple into my arms and took a couple of the bags from Finley. "Fine by me. Let's roll, baby."

Chapter Fourteen

Finley

When we reached the handsome Craftsman-style house faced in creamy natural stone, its deep wooden eaves seemed to reach out to shelter us. My stomach settled the tiniest bit. Grey turned and pulled his black SUV into its two-car garage. As we unloaded the car, it suddenly struck me that I'd never seen Grey's home before. *How strange.* That night when we'd first run into each other at the strip club had been over a month ago. And it was starting to feel like he'd been part of our lives forever. So how was it that he'd always come to us, never the other way around?

But even more striking was the house itself. I looked around in awe as Grey led us to our guest bedroom upstairs. The huge kitchen boasted speckled granite countertops, stainless steel fixtures, and an island where I could picture Maple sitting in her high chair to watch me cook. The first floor's sliding glass doors led out onto a broad cedar deck overlooking the lush green lawn—impressive, considering northeast Texas's brutal summers. In one corner stood a sprawling fifteen-foot pecan tree; in the other, a pool glimmered bright blue, safely fenced off with a black wrought iron gate. Upstairs, the master bathroom was dominated by a long, deep soaking tub that Maple would love at bath time. I fantasized briefly about melting into its soothing hot water myself. I floated through the house in a fog, wondering if this was all real. It seemed too good to be true.

Grey laid our bags on the bed, then turned to rest his hand on my shoulder. "I'll go get the last few things out of the car. You two just make yourselves at home, okay?"

I suddenly couldn't trust my voice to stay steady. "Sure," I muttered, not sure whether that tight note was bitterness or grief or simple exhaustion.

Grey paused a moment, watching my face, then nodded and went back downstairs. His footsteps on the hardwood faded, leaving me alone with the dark pit in my stomach. The notion of playing house here seemed too ... I didn't know the word. Presumptuous? Inappropriate?

This place was almost as spacious and beautiful as Brant's mountain lodge. Grey had obviously done well for himself after quitting the SEALs. My pride twinged. I couldn't deny that this was a better environment for Maple than anything I could have provided on my own.

My eyes grew misty as I folded our clothes into the dresser and hung them in the closet. I could hear Maple scuffling and giggling as she explored under the bed. Everything was just so unfair. *This* was the life we should have had. The house I'd bought with Marcus could have been just as nice as Grey's was. It had held all of our hopes and dreams. The big family we'd planned for, the untroubled childhood that Maple deserved. Instead, she got a terrible mother who couldn't take care of her own fucking daughter without handouts. No matter how hard I tried, it just wasn't good enough. I wasn't good enough. And I was starting to fear that I might never be.

Get a grip, Finley. Having a pity party won't help anyone. I knew I was just feeling sorry for myself. The last few days would shake anyone's confidence. But those pathetic thoughts kept pouring through my mind like a flash flood, muddy and dangerous and unstoppably fast. I should have tried harder. I hadn't truly done my best. Every small moment of weakness—buying convenience food instead of cooking, sleeping instead of working, letting my fake smile slip while I was on the clock—was another dollar I'd stolen from Maple's future.

But dear God, I was just so mind-bogglingly tired. None of my struggling and scraping ever seemed to make any progress. Was there even any point of trying to climb out of this hole? Life would just slap me right back down again. *Heads, reality wins. Tails, I lose.*

Too late, I heard footsteps stop at the bedroom doorway. "Fin?"

I quickly glanced out the window, trying to hide my tears while pretending to admire the prairie view. "Y-yeah?"

Grey didn't buy my calm act for a second. I could hear it in his deep, solemn sigh. But he didn't push me to talk about why I felt so upset; he already knew damn well what was wrong. Instead, he held out his phone and said, "Call the strip club and quit."

Shocked, I spun around, forgetting my tear-stained cheeks. "What? Why?"

"Because you're not going back there."

"I can't just—"

His eyes hardened. But behind them, something almost like fear flickered. "Because it exposed you to low-lifes and creeps without even paying you enough to live on. You can do better."

Patronizing prick. I squared my jaw right back at him. "Who says I can? You don't know my life story. In two years of job hunting, that place was the best I ever found. It *worked* for us. Where else would let me stay at home with Maple during the day?"

"You can do better," he repeated simply.

Taking a deep breath, I balled up every ounce of wounded pride I'd ever felt and threw it in his face. "Not everyone can afford to turn up their noses at perfectly good work."

That was kind of a low blow. I didn't give a shit. But apparently, neither did Grey. He just shook his head, still holding out the phone.

Was he not even going to listen to me anymore? Blood pounding in my ears, I hissed so Maple wouldn't hear, "And what the hell would I do if I *did* quit? You think unemployment is better than stripping? Safer? More dignified?"

"I'll help you," he insisted, voice rising a little.

I shook my head savagely. "No way. I might be okay with hiding out here for a little while, but we won't mooch off of you. I'll buy our own food and diapers and pay a fair share of the rest. And I'll need a job to do that."

For a long moment, Grey stared at me, searching my eyes. Could he sense my desperation? He had to understand why independence was so important to me. I'd already lost everything else in my life; if I lost this battle, too, I wouldn't even know who I was anymore.

Finally, he sighed again, yielding ground. "Fine. I understand. I'll work something out."

I cocked my head, eyes narrowing slightly. "Like what?" I wasn't about to let him decide some crazy scheme for me.

He raked his fingers through his short black hair with an exasperated noise. "Fin, please. Do you trust me?"

I considered for a minute. After the daring rescue he'd just pulled off, I really did. In fact, I had to admit...I might trust him more than anyone else on Earth. Which caused a fresh round of tears to fill my eyes.

At my reluctant nod, he thrust out the phone again. "Good. Then call the club."

I took the phone and dialed. It rang a few times. Then, over a thumping bass line, a familiar brisk voice answered, "Hello, this is the Dolly House. How can I help you?"

I licked my suddenly dry lips. "Ginger?"

A moment of stony silence. I would have thought the line had gone dead if it weren't for the music blaring in the background. Maple chose that moment to wriggle out from under the bed, full of curiosity. Grey immediately scooped her up and distracted her with quiet murmurs.

When Ginger spoke again, her chirpy customer-service tone had vanished into genuine warmth. "Finley? Oh my goodness. I can't tell you what a relief it is to hear from you. When you missed all your shifts—you never miss work, dear—and then that cute soldier came around looking for you, I was so worried. What happened? Was it Brant?"

"I..." The last thing I wanted to do was relive the past week. "Y-yes, I had some trouble with Brant. But it's all over now."

"Oh my goodness," she gasped again. "What a horrible little man. I should have known he'd do something crazy someday. I just thought you were his favorite, but the way he always hovered around you wasn't healthy—"

Unable to wait any longer, I broke in. "I'm sorry, Ginger. I'd rather not get into the whole story right now." Possibly not ever. "The reason I called is...I'm quitting."

Silence again. Then a rush of static as Ginger sighed into the receiver. "I see. Well, dear, the girls and I will certainly miss you. Especially Layla."

Something oddly like nostalgia twinged in my chest. I'd miss all of them right back. Working at the club hadn't always been a barrel of laughs—to put it mildly—but I had met some great people there.

"But I'm glad you've moved on to greener pastures," Ginger continued. "Nobody wants to stay in a place like this forever." She gave a little cackle. "Except for me, of course. You girls are like family to me. But that's exactly my point. Children are meant to grow up and leave you."

I found myself smiling even as I blinked back tears. "Thank you, Ginger. You've always been so wonderful."

"It's my job, dear. Take care now."

Swallowing hard, I hit the red END icon and handed the phone back to Grey. "I'm done."

He nodded soberly. "It'll be okay, I promise."

Maple looked back and forth between us, sensing the negative mood, and started squirming for freedom. Grey let her down onto the bed. As I stroked Maple's soft, fine hair, Grey dialed another number. I didn't think too hard about what he was doing until he said, "Good afternoon, Mr. Barton. I was wondering...were we still looking for an administrative assistant?"

My eyes went wide. "A what now?" I spluttered. "Grey, I'm not trained for—"

The infuriating asshole actually held up his hand to shush me. "Great. That's perfect. And she can work from home, right?" He paused. "That should be fine. Yes, Mrs. Sutton can start tomorrow. Thank you." He hung up and raised his eyebrows at me. "There, see? What'd I tell you? You're Redstone's newest employee. You'll have to attend our Friday meetings, but I figured with your new salary, you can afford a babysitter for a couple hours once a week. And you can use my laptop until you can buy your own."

I wanted to slap that self-satisfied smirk right off Grey's face. I wanted to kiss him until neither of us could breathe. Instead, I laughed out loud, shaking my head. "You're a real pain in the...the hindquarters, you know that, right?"

Grey shrugged, still grinning. "I try my best," he said. "I've got to go into the office for a little while. I probably won't be back in time for dinner. Feel free to order takeout or help yourself to whatever's in the fridge."

I nodded. Some time alone would do me good. In fact... "I was thinking me and Maple could go for a swim, if that's okay."

"Of course. You guys deserve a little fun. Just make sure you lock all the doors and keep your cell handy."

My eyes flitted around the room and my chest tightened again.

"Hey," he murmured, reaching out to stroke my cheek. "I didn't mean it like that. I'm just overprotective. Now that I have you here ..." His voice went stiff and he paused. "You'll be safe here, I promise."

I believed him. Every last word. And for a person who was normally pretty stoic, I was turning into a fucking waterworks factory. Blinking back tears, I simply nodded.

***

After I watched his SUV back out into the street and disappear, I dressed myself and Maple in our new swimsuits, fitted a pair of water wings over her arms, and took her downstairs. She ran in clumsy, excited circles around me as I walked out into the backyard and unlatched the pool's gate.

We sat down to play on the steps of the shallow end. The

late summer sun warmed my hair and shoulders as the cool water lapped around my legs. Its chlorine smell reminded me of childhood swimming lessons in the city pool. Just beyond the back fence, I could hear the tall wild grasses rustling in the breeze, like the open range itself was shushing my fears. With a giddy, gap-toothed grin, Maple kicked and slapped at the water, letting out joyful squeals. Her baby giggles were contagious and I found myself smiling and laughing along with her.

Within half an hour, I felt like a different person. Fun, relaxed, carefree. I wished I could be this version of myself more often. I hated that I'd been so stressed out and angry and tearful for so long. Grey was right—Maple deserved better. And, I realized with sudden clarity, so did I.

When Marcus and I had decided to have children, I'd committed to putting myself second for the rest of my life. And I was fine with that. It was my choice; I didn't resent or regret it. But it hadn't left much room for thinking about what I deserved. Especially not when Marcus died and I found myself the family's only breadwinner. We'd had no time or money for luxuries. Even when I found myself with spare cash, I never spent it on myself. It always felt so frivolous. More than frivolous— downright wrong, like I was taking food out of Maple's mouth.

So it didn't matter what I deserved. It didn't matter what was fair. All I could let myself have was what I absolutely needed in order to keep functioning.

But I'd learned that I *did* need those little treats every once in a while. Like the surprise spa day that Grey had convinced me to take. That kind of self-care was almost as important as sleeping and eating right. If I didn't feed my soul, it would starve to death. And that wouldn't be fair to Maple or myself. She deserved a fun, relaxed mom...and I deserved to be happy.

That first idea was fairly obvious, but the second was revolutionary. It never would have occurred to me before Grey changed our lives. I always thought about Maple, so it fell to Grey to think about *me*. He helped me without asking for anything in return. And it wasn't just about the money he'd saved us—all the dinners and toys and small favors. He chased my worries away and gave me permission to enjoy life. He brought me a kind of peace I hadn't felt in a long time.

I let Maple splash around in the pool for a little while longer. Then I took her back inside and gave her a quick bath to rinse off the chlorine. I couldn't have her pale blonde hair turning green. I decided to start cooking dinner early. Whenever Grey came home, I wanted to be ready for a long talk.

Chapter Fifteen

Greyson

I was done. I was done hoping and praying for something that would never happen. Done pining over a beautiful woman I would obviously never have. Late that night, hoping Finley was already in bed, I let myself inside quietly. I'd worked for several hours this afternoon, trying to get caught up on everything after being out on assignment the past several days. That assignment being, saving the life of the woman and child who were currently asleep under my roof.

I toed off my boots and set my keys and phone on the table beside the door. The soft glow from the lamp in the living room illuminated my path and I went to turn it off before heading upstairs. Instead, I found Finley curled up on the sofa, a glass of red wine in hand. Her hair was damp from the shower and she was dressed in a pair of yoga pants that hugged her curves, along with a tank top. No bra.

Fuck.

Having her this close was going to be torture. I'd be jacking off more than a horny teenager if she was going to prance around wearing shit like that.

"Hi," she offered. Her voice was light, almost shy. Her

anger and sadness from earlier seemed to be gone.

"Thought you'd be in bed by now."

"I wanted to enjoy the peace and quiet. Would you like to join me for a glass of wine?"

"Uh...sure," I stumbled over my words.

While I sat down, Finley poured wine into a second glass on the coffee table. *Was she waiting for me to get home?*

I accepted the glass of wine and took a sip. "Did you guys have a good day?"

Finley nodded. "We swam and played outside, and then I made us pasta for dinner."

"Sorry." I rubbed the back of my neck. "I probably didn't have much in the way of groceries. We can fix that tomorrow."

She reached out and touched my hand. "You've done enough. Please don't beat yourself up about the groceries. Plus, I found the good stuff." She raised her wine glass and took a sip.

We sipped our wine in comfortable silence while I filled her in on the latest news concerning Brant. An officer would be coming over tomorrow to take her statement and I'd learned that not only would Brant be prosecuted for the kidnapping, but he was wanted for embezzling from his company, too.

"In other words, he's going to go away for a long time," I summed up. "You're safe."

Finley smiled warmly at me. "Thank you."

"You know I'd do anything for you and Maple."

"I'm starting to sense that."

"I would have been there for you a lot sooner if I'd known … I didn't know how bad things had gotten. I knew you were fiercely protective of your way of life, but I still should have come to check on you sooner. It was total blind luck that I stumbled across you in the club that night."

"That night you admitted you got excited watching me dance." She grinned. Apparently the wine had loosened her tongue along with her frayed nerves.

"Hell yeah, I did. I was hard as a fucking rock." And I was getting there now, just remembering the way she'd moved.

Finley's tongue poked out to wet her bottom lip and her pulse pumped faster in her neck. "I don't know how to do this, Grey. Even if I wanted to."

I moved closer to her on the couch. "The first step is for you to stop hating me. I do that enough for the both of us." And I had come to realize just how pointless and sick that self-hatred really was. For the past two years, I'd shut myself away, denied myself any real closure, alternating between avoiding my guilt and stewing in it. No matter how much I punished myself, it wouldn't bring Marcus back from the dead—but I couldn't imagine forgiving myself, either. That would have felt like a betrayal. Like dodging my responsibility as the leader of our assault team. So I'd just kept pouring salt in my own wounds, letting them fester.

A few weeks with Finley and Maple had taught me something I couldn't learn in two whole years alone. Before I knew it, being part of their little family had started to cleanse me. Ironic, considering whose widow Finley was and how she used to feel about me. But I could tell that she had changed, too. A new softness was written in her eyes.

"I don't hate you," she murmured, her gaze drifting down to her wine glass.

I tipped her chin up with two fingers. "I'm sorry, can you say that a little louder?"

I expected her to roll her eyes, instead she gazed deep into mine. "How could I still hate you? After everything you've done for me, for my child?"

"Because of what happened with Marcus," I said, knowing the mood needed to take a darker turn before we found the light again. Together, I hoped.

"What happened was an accident. I've come to accept

that."

I nodded. "I did everything I could to try and save him."

"I know that now. I'm sorry I've dumped extra guilt on you." Biting her lip, she heaved in a deep sigh through her nose. "I've been thinking about it, and I realized...a big part of the reason I hated you was because anger was easier to deal with than sadness and fear. I wanted someone to pin the blame on. Something to *do*, somewhere to point my feelings. I couldn't accept blind fate."

"You were grieving, Finley. It's okay." God knew I'd struggled with the idea of a world where terrible things just *happened* sometimes, snatching people up without rhyme or reason.

"Thanks. Maybe it was okay...for a while. But it's past time to move on." Her mouth was set tight, her green eyes shining with tears and the determination I'd come to admire so much. This woman had serious grit. When she decided something, then that was that.

We each took a deep breath. This conversation had been almost two long years in the making, and now, somehow we were tiptoeing our way through it unscathed.

Finley cleared her throat. "So ... assuming I don't hate you, what's the next step?"

I could hardly believe it. She was handing me an olive branch. She was taking a step, making the first move, and it was exactly what I needed. I'd put myself out there so many times, only for her to pull away. This time needed to be different. She had to take a couple steps forward to show me that all my efforts weren't in vain – that she wasn't only living here because she was out of options. This needed to be about *me* and the man I was. I needed her to want me, not just need me.

My heart kicked up speed in my chest and I moved a little closer. "The next step is that we take this slow. See where it goes."

She laughed. "Greyson. We don't have to take things *that* slow. I had a baby. I was a stripper."

We had talked about the past enough for tonight. That much, we could agree on. Now it was time to focus on the present, her heated glance, her slightly mischievous smile, her body just waiting for my touch.

"Even if we don't go slow, you deserve someone who's willing to—who's *happy* to, if that's what you need. Someone who'll treat you like a goddess. Someone steady who will be there when shit gets tough."

"Slow and steady, huh?" She smiled warmly at me.

"Maple deserves slow and steady, too."

"You're too good to us."

I stroked her cheek with the pad of my thumb. "I won't rush this or fuck it up. I want to take my time and love you in all the ways you deserve."

Her breath hitched in her throat and she made a little satisfied noise. She hadn't felt this type of need and longing in a long time. Neither had I. And she was looking at me like she was seeing me for the first time. Her eyes were two huge pools of desire, and the urge to give her everything she subconsciously dreamed of was a raw need pulsing through me.

I took the wine glass from her hand and set it on the table with mine. Then I leaned in and took her mouth like I'd been craving. Hot. Hungry and desperate. There was nothing slow about it—we'd been building toward this moment for too long. She whimpered softly and clutched at my shirt with her fists. I cradled her jaw in my hands, my mouth remaining fused to hers. My tongue lapped slow circles around hers and Finley moaned into my kiss, angling her body closer. I needed her closer. I needed more. And I wasn't stopping until she told me to.

I broke away for just a second. "Come here." Hauling her across the couch, I placed her in my lap, then gripped her ass, grinding my erection into the warm cleft between her legs. We simultaneously groaned. I knew it would only be a matter of time before I was peeling down her yoga pants and sinking into her warmth. But first, I needed to force myself to slow down. I took a deep breath and moved from her lips to her neck, dropping wet kisses against her silky skin. She deserved to be worshiped and loved – every inch of her.

"Greyson ..." she moaned, tilting her neck back to give me better access.

Gently sinking my teeth into her skin, I nibbled along the column of her throat.

"Is this crazy ... me and you...?" she moaned again.

"Doesn't feel crazy, sweetheart. Feels fucking perfect." I pressed my cock up again, and she circled her hips over me.

"Yeah," she breathed, pressing her mouth against my neck this time, taking a taste.

When she pulled back, I lifted her shirt over her head and tossed it to the floor. Her bare breasts were high and proud, topped with rosy nipples. Leaning down, I took one in my mouth, swirling my tongue over the peak and sucking it gently. She was so responsive and ready; her low moan pierced straight through me. I massaged both breasts in my hands, my thumbs raking over her nipples as she trembled and whimpered.

She silently placed her hand over the front of my pants, palming my erection.

As good as her touch felt, I pulled her hand away. "Stand

up."

She rose from my lap and stood before me. I peeled her yoga pants and panties down her legs until she stepped out of them and stood before me. Between her legs was shaved bare and delicate folds exposed her swollen clit.

I pulled her back into my lap, and her hands immediately went to work on my belt buckle. Her delicate hands freed me from the confines of my boxers and then she suddenly stopped.

"Jesus, Grey," she muttered, her voice filled with surprise.

"What – I ..." I looked down and saw her view. My cock was so hard and so swollen – standing tall and ready.

"Take me in your hand, baby," I murmured, kissing her lips, then watching to see that she did.

As she tentatively curled one small fist around me, my breath caught in my throat. She moved her hand up and down, her thumb catching the drop of fluid at the tip.

She pushed her hips closer to rub her warm, wet cunt over the base of my shaft.

A strangled groan rumbled in my chest. Nothing had ever felt as good as her slick folds working up and down against me. I thumbed her clit, sucked on her nipples while she continued rubbing her wet pussy all over me.

"Greyson ..." she moaned.

Using her own moisture, I circled her sensitive bud with my thumb. She watched – transfixed, her eyes wide and wild. Continuing to play with her clit, I licked and nibbled her breasts and felt her start to buck against me. *Bingo.* "Come for me, sweetheart," I whispered. A second later Finley gave a little shout and a rush of warmth coated my cock.

I slowed my movements, my thumb carefully pressing down, and watched. Breathless, Finley's movement slowed and became frantic and jerky. Her juices were all over me and it was warm, silky perfection. As good as it felt, I knew it could feel even better. I needed to be inside of her. I lifted her ass over me, depositing her right over the top of my cock. Her gaze latched on to mine and she understood what I needed. Lowering herself onto me, Finley's eyes met mine as our bodies joined for the first time.

I'd never made love like this – face to face, gazes locked. But rather than it feeling intrusive, too bold, it felt just right. I wouldn't want it any other way. Those emerald eyes were locked on mine and I could see everything she was thinking and feeling. Desire. Fear. *Love.*

"Hang on, baby."

Finley gripped my shoulders and I began to move. I thrust with deep, powerful strokes, unable to hold back, fucking her hard and fast, claiming her as my own. She cried out and soon, I found the spot that made her body clench around me. She came again, hard, clawing at my back and repeating my name over and over again. The desperate way her inner muscles pulsed around me pushed me over the edge, and I let go with a groan.

As perfect as that hard and fast fuck on the couch had felt, I needed her closer, so I'd carried her up to my room, and placed her on the bed. She looked like a goddess, so elegant and beautiful spread out on my pillow. I couldn't stop myself from worshipping her again. We made love twice more that night, slow and passionately, and it was as close as I'd ever felt to anyone ever before.

Chapter Sixteen

Finley

Someone was moving around downstairs. Hearing muted voices and the occasional clank, I stirred, twisting the sheets around me. It took me a moment to realize that I was in Grey's bed—and buck naked. I squinted at the clock radio to see that it was after ten. I hadn't slept so late or so long in almost two years. I sighed with pleasure as I stretched, feeling incredibly rested.

My memories of last night soon returned like a warm rain. Grey had been so sweet...and such an amazing lover. As I rolled out of bed, I winced a little, feeling the strain in my hips and thighs and the pleasant soreness between them. I giggled to myself. Dancing had kept me pretty damn fit, but it had been a long time since those particular muscles had gotten so much exercise.

I still felt languid from my great night—both the asleep and awake parts. Wanting to savor this lazy-Sunday-morning feeling, I shrugged on Grey's plaid terrycloth robe instead of getting dressed. It was more than a little loose on me, hanging off my shoulders to offer an eyeful of cleavage, but nobody would be seeing anything they hadn't seen before. And I liked the idea of distracting Grey from whatever the hell he was up to.

I walked downstairs to find Grey and Maple in the kitchen. Grey stood in front of the stove, tossing a huge wok of sliced chicken and vegetables. My stomach growled at the spicy, peanutty smell. In her high chair, near the breakfast nook's table, Maple was playing with a plateful of small chicken chunks and carrot coins. When she saw me in the doorway, she squealed with excitement and hurled a baby corncob at the floor so hard it bounced.

"Well, good morning to you, too." I crossed the kitchen to kiss Maple's forehead hello.

"You got one of those for me?" Grey called.

I sauntered over to him, leaned in, and placed an exaggeratedly chaste peck on his cheek. His wry grin made it clear that he'd collect what I owed him later...and then some. *Ooh.*

Letting my shoulder brush his, I watched the colorful bell peppers, carrots, snow peas, and broccoli dance in the wok. "So what's the occasion?"

"Making lunch," he replied. Admirably, his eyes only dipped to my chest for an instant. I'd have to do a better job tempting him. "Don't worry, I served Maple her share before adding the hot chili oil."

I laughed. "Lunch? It's ten in the morning."

Grey turned his head so that his full lips skimmed my cheek as he spoke. His freshly shaven skin was so soft; I couldn't decide which I liked better, smooth Grey or stubbly Grey. "Yes, but we've been up since five-thirty, so breakfast was at six. Now we're hungry again."

God, I'm already in so deep. Just hearing him say "we" like that made me feel all warm and fuzzy inside. And neither of us seemed to be able to stop touching each other. But yikes, five-thirty in the morning? Had Maple woken him up? How had I slept through that? Sex with Greyson must have worn me out more than I'd realized. I supposed six powerful orgasms could do that to a girl ... or he just had a magical cock. Pulling myself from *that* daydream, I realized he was still watching me.

"You didn't have to take care of everything yourself," I said, faintly embarrassed that he'd been doing all my work for me. "I'm sorry. Do you want to grab a nap? I can take over."

He shook his head. "I want to do this, Fin. Let me in, okay?"

Caught off guard by the sudden lump in my throat, I nodded my permission instead of speaking aloud. My eyes stung a little. But these weren't the kind of tears I'd become all too used to fighting. They were happy tears. It's like my life had pulled a one-eighty, in the best possible way. I'd never imagined getting a second chance at a happily ever after – I thought those only came about once. And with Greyson Archer, no less?

A quiet beep made me turn my head. There was a deluxe rice cooker by the sink, opposite the kitchen's stove side, and its light was flashing. I took off the lid, inhaling the jasmine-scented steam that billowed from the fluffy white grains.

"If you're dying to help, the dishes are in the cupboard just to your left," I heard Grey say.

I found two wide bowls, heaped rice into each one, and placed them on the counter at Grey's elbow. I added a couple cooled spoonfuls to Maple's plate and she promptly mushed her hands into the soft white stuff like modeling clay. As I filled our water glasses, Grey brought the bowls to the table, now piled high with spicy peanut stir-fry. My mouth watered. This was a weird breakfast for me, but it looked and smelled so amazing that I didn't care.

"So," Grey declared as we sat down, "what's on the agenda? I've taken the whole day off. We can do whatever you want."

My mind instinctively started calculating how many hours I had left until my shift, whether we needed anything from the store, how I would handle dinner. Then I remembered: I'd quit my job yesterday. And I didn't start my new one until Monday. Grey's fridge and pantry were fully stocked. I didn't even need to cook.

My free time was, in fact, free. I actually *could* do whatever I wanted.

...What did normal people do on their days off? I was drawing a blank. This whole arrangement would take some getting used to.

"Maple loved playing in the pool yesterday," I mused, raising a forkful of food to my lips. "Maybe we could do that."

"Sounds good to me," Grey said. "That thing has sat empty for so long, it'll be good to see it get some use." Then his warm smile turned sly. "But make sure you're ready to go out at five tonight. I've got a surprise for you."

***

"I wish you'd told me we were going to Doma Vaquera," I said as soon as the waiter had left with our orders. I awkwardly smoothed my faded cotton miniskirt as far down my lap as it would go, then gave up and draped my napkin to cover the rest of me. "I would've dressed nicer. I feel so out of place."

"Don't worry, babe. This place isn't *that* fancy...and you look beautiful. Nobody would ever think you didn't belong here." Grey raised his eyebrows in a way that added: *And if anyone implies otherwise, I'll examine their eyes with my fist.*

My stomach gave a hot little flip and I couldn't help but smile. Damn his stupid sexy voice, telling me exactly what I wanted to hear. I hadn't had a man in my life for so long, all his sweet declarations were making me melt.

At five o'clock sharp, Nolan and his new fiancée had knocked on our front door. They had introduced themselves as Maple's new babysitters. Sensing that I was about to protest, Grey had pulled me aside and checked that I was okay. I thought it over and nodded my consent. I knew Nolan well – he'd been one of my husband's closest friends. And based on the stories I'd heard from Grey about Lacey, she was a sweetheart. And they already had Maple giggling in the other room. So I'd let Grey sweep me into his car and on our way to the swankiest steakhouse in town, with tickets to the theater for later.

Dinner and a movie. Our first official date together was sweet and simple. But I hadn't done anything like this in so long—and it meant so much. I let out a quiet chuckle.

He cocked his head slightly. "What's funny?"

"I was just thinking...we've done our whole relationship backwards, haven't we?" I teased. "First raising Maple together, then sleeping together, then dating."

I'd only been joking. But his smile faded instantly.

Shit. The last thing I'd wanted was to hurt his feelings. "Oh, Grey, I didn't mean..."

He reached across the table to take my hands. "I know," he

said soberly. "I'm sorry our road's been so rocky. You deserve better. So from now on, I'm going to do this thing right."

I bit my lip, willing myself not to choke up in front of the whole restaurant. I hadn't known just how badly I wanted that until he said it. Something normal, something easy. A man treating me like a woman. Greyson Archer specifically, clearing a space in his life just for me.

"So, Finley..." Still holding my hands, Grey slid out of his seat and onto one knee, startling me. "Will you be my girlfriend?"

I couldn't breathe. "G-get off the floor, you big crazy man," I stuttered, the urges to laugh and cry welling up at the same time. "People are going to think you're..." I couldn't say the word *proposing*.

Chuckling, he finally let go of my hands and sat back in his chair. "Sorry. It felt like the right thing to do in the moment."

He sure didn't look sorry. I rolled my eyes—but I couldn't wipe the huge, stupid grin off my face.

And it wasn't as if I could say no to this man. Even when I'd been cold and aloof to him, he'd still been part of our lives – under the guise of being there for Maple, when in reality, that was one of the things that had won me over in the first place.

"Is that a yes?" he prompted. "I promise you won't regret

it."

His earnest desire stole my breath away. I let myself giggle like a schoolgirl, joy surging through me. "Sure. I'm all yours."

That wasn't entirely true; a part of me still belonged to Marcus. But for the first time, I wanted to change that. I wanted to let Grey have a piece of me, too. I could see the path ahead and I knew, deep in my bones, that it was the right one. We'd get to the end when we were ready.

Grey's dark eyes flashed. "Oh, you shouldn't have said that," he murmured, his voice low and sinful. "Now I'll never let you out of my bed tonight."

A whisper of heat pulsed through me. Suddenly I wasn't sure if I wanted to sit through dinner and an entire movie. But I knew that the wait, the anticipation, would just make this evening's grand finale even more satisfying. And it gave me time to plan my own surprise.

***

We didn't get back home until eleven. After we thanked Nolan and Lacey, then checked that Maple was sound asleep in her crib, I told Grey to wait for me on his bed. He obeyed—though not without stealing a toe-curling kiss first. I dug through my closet in the guest room with a naughty thrill. I may not have been a stripper anymore, but I'd kept all my dancing gear, and I vividly remembered how Grey had devoured me with his eyes on that first night. I would give him his own private show again. And this time, I'd go all-out.

I wriggled into my outfit—a matching set of crimson lace panties, stockings, garter belt, and push-up bra—and refreshed my makeup, letting my hair flow over my shoulders. As I sauntered into Grey's room, I faltered for a split second at the luscious sight before me. Grey had taken off his shirt and was reclining like a Greek god on his bed, sculpted and sensual. *Holy hell. How does he look so good just lying there like that?* My mouth somehow watered and went dry at the same time.

Luckily, Grey was even more stunned than me. He sat bolt upright. "Jesus...you look like a dream come true, baby."

I quickly picked my jaw up off the floor and got back to business. "Always glad to hear from a fan, Mister Archer," I purred. Slowly I came closer, swaying my hips, letting him admire my round, toned ass and deep cleavage. "Now sit back, relax, and enjoy...but no touching."

"Fuck, Fin, you're going to kill me," he said.

I gave a throaty chuckle, my pride thoroughly stroked, even though I wanted my "customer" just as badly as he wanted me. There was no telling whose willpower would give out first...but either way, I was betting it wouldn't take long.

I closed my eyes for a moment to call up the memory of

my favorite routine. I heard that old familiar song in my mind—
a story of dangerous seduction, electric guitar riffs like cries of
pleasure. I let its sultry rhythm roll through my body in sinuous
waves. Raising my arms to flaunt my breasts, I tossed my head
back, running my hands through my long blonde hair. I could
feel Grey's eyes burning on my skin.

This right here was what I loved about dancing. I could
forget everything about the outside world and just live in the
moment, rejoicing in my body. My blood sang hot with the
music's beat. I was falling under my own spell—all the good
parts of working at the club, with none of the bad. And it was
time to start my routine's main attraction.

Still rocking my hips to the beat, I gradually turned around,
hugging myself. My hands slid up the curve of my waist and
stopped at my bra's clasp. One by one, I undid the tiny hooks,
until the bra hung only by its straps. I paused to let them slide
from my shoulders. Finally, with a coy glance over my shoulder,
I tossed the bra into the corner of the room. By the time I
completed my excruciatingly slow turn, I was topless—but I
kept my hands covering my breasts.

Grey's tongue snuck out to wet his lower lip. I wasn't sure
if he realized he'd done it, but the thought of him losing even
that small amount of control just excited me more.

"You fucking tease," he groaned.

I giggled. "That's generally the idea of a strip*tease*, soldier.

You want to see?"

"Jesus, who wouldn't?"

With a smirk, I replied, "Flattery will get you everywhere," and I slowly let my hands drop.

This time Grey made a show of licking his lips. I remembered how good his mouth had felt on my breasts before, and the tension between my thighs curled tighter. God, I was sopping wet already. And he could probably tell, with how skimpy this thong was...*no, no, don't think about that yet.* I still wanted to finish the foreplay I'd planned. The time to rip off his pants and free that monster of an erection would come soon enough.

I turned around and ground my ass into his lap. I knew how much he liked my ass—and avoiding looking at his handsome face and sexy, rippling muscles would help me control myself. But I could still feel his huge, straining bulge. I could hear him, too, and his husky groan shot white-hot sparks straight to my clit. Damn, maybe I couldn't wait after all.

Getting close to him again, I murmured into his ear, "You ever wonder what happens in the champagne room?" I was totally bluffing, I didn't know either.

"I take it you're going to show me," he replied. I shivered at the rough note in his voice, he was just barely restraining himself.

Kneeling on the bed to straddle his toned thighs, I ran my hands up my stomach and over my breasts. My nipples were already so stiff, even that slight touch zinged through me. I pinched them and ground against his bulge just to hear him moan again. If he hadn't been able to tell how wet I was before, he sure as hell knew now. Then I reached between my legs and unzipped his fly. His cock sprang out, hard as steel, its head glistening. I ran my thumb through the slick wetness of his excitement. I could feel our pulses throbbing together where my clit touched his hot shaft.

"Finley..." he groaned.

The desperation in his voice made me look up—and then I was lost forever. His eyes grabbed mine, holding them fast as he said, "You're so beautiful. Perfect inside and out."

It was such a serious, honest declaration, so heavy with longing, that it knocked me breathless, leaving me flushed and dizzy. "Grey..."

"And now that you're mine I'm going to worship you."

My heart quickened at the raw need in his voice. What drove him was so much more than simple lust. His whole being, body and soul, was focused on me. This was going to be the ride of my life—and I couldn't wait a single second longer.

I fumbled to grab a condom from his nightstand drawer and roll it on, as we decided together that we better start using those, at least for now. Then I yanked aside the crotch of my panties and sank down onto his thick cock, groaning aloud at the burning stretch, the sensation of fullness that promised so much pleasure. Fuck, how had I survived without this for two whole years? With a growl of triumph, Grey flipped us over and drove into me. I kissed him hard to let his mouth muffle my greedy cries.

We made fierce love—not impersonal screwing, but not slow and sweet, either. We had denied ourselves too long for that. We were starving, and we wolfed down our fill of each other. His hips pistoned faster as I urged him on with mewling moans, overwhelmed yet still needing more. Each thrust hit deep and hard enough to make my head spin. The fiery pleasure built higher, hotter...Then suddenly flared, flooding heat from my core all through my body. My eyes flew open in shock as I trembled and spasmed around him. I'd never come so easily before. Yet here I was, exploding like a supernova without a direct touch on my clit. And the tension immediately began to wind up again. *Jesus, what's this man done to me?*

Greyson was searing hot and achingly tender all at once. His long, thick cock rubbed sensitive spots I didn't even know I owned. He knew what I needed without my having to ask, and he gave it to me without expecting anything in return. Just one meaningful glance from him could make filthy thoughts rush into my head. And I felt so safe around Grey. I knew he would never judge me or put his desires before mine. I could let myself go, fully and completely, and trust him to catch me.

"One more time, baby," Grey growled. "Come for me. You can do it."

My pussy clenched when his fingers brushed my clit. All it took was a few rubs of that swollen, slick bud. Once again, my legs tightened around his hips and my nails dug into his back. I almost sobbed at the pleasure washing through my oversensitive flesh.

"I'm never letting you go," Grey panted harshly. Then he bit his lip and groaned aloud with release, his cock throbbing deep inside me.

I collapsed bonelessly when he pulled out, as if he'd been the only thing keeping me up. He threw away the condom and lay down beside me. I kissed the SEAL trident tattoo on his bicep, then squirmed close to pillow my head on his strong arm. I inhaled his masculine scent, sweat and sex and musky cologne; his chest hair tickled my nose.

I had meant to take off the rest of my lingerie at some point. But I was so exhausted, so satisfied and warm. We fell asleep with our legs entwined.

Chapter Seventeen

Greyson

For the last six weeks, my world had revolved around my two leading ladies. Six weeks of family dinners, of Finley sleeping in my bed each night, of simple pleasures like playing tag in the backyard and shopping for fruit at the farmer's market. It was a small slice of heaven that I hadn't experienced in a long time. Or maybe ever.

I felt better than I had in years. My step was lighter, laughter came easier. I generally just felt more rested and at peace than ever before. Who knew being in love would do that to a man? It certainly explained a few things—like how my buddy Nolan's life magically transformed from a sworn bachelor playing the field to laying aside all his bad habits for the right girl. There was not a damn thing wrong with monogamy in my book. Two people who loved and trusted each other enough to stick together through all of life's ups and downs was something to be cherished.

And Finley? She'd transitioned into her new life beautifully, even better than I could have hoped for. She worked part time for Redstone from my home office we'd fixed up for her with a new laptop. We bought a desk in cream-colored wood, light gray gauzy curtains, and a tufted purple armchair. She'd definitely taken it to heart when I told her to make it *her* office. She'd even hung a couple of framed photos. My favorite was a painting with various sayings about strength and determination and having the courage to live your dreams – even though the damn thing was hot pink. Her new position at Redstone had her fielding phone calls, typing up memos, and handling the business expenses and reimbursements. She'd impressed Jerry Barton right away with her attention to detail and initiative. He didn't need to know that office work was a far cry from what was on her past resume. These days, she danced only for me.

Maple was thriving, too. She was enrolled at a nearby preschool for the couple half days that Finley worked. She'd caught onto everything so quickly, trying to sing along to her ABCs and everything.

Life was pretty close to perfect. Except ...

I couldn't help the pit of dread churning in my stomach. Today was the two-year anniversary of Marcus' death.

I left a single light pink rose on Finley's bedside table and left before sun up. It wasn't my busy work obligations driving me – it was fear. I couldn't face her this morning. It was one of the most important dates in her life. Right up there with the day Maple was born, the day she lost her husband would always be burned into her brain, just like it was in mine.

I'd left the long-stemmed rose, its color signifying

sympathy, along with a note:

I'll be thinking of you today.

And then I'd escaped into the darkness like a coward. Again. I didn't know the right things to say, didn't know the pretty words that could soothe her heartache and the gigantic hole his loss had left.

I'd been at work for several long, distracted hours when it suddenly struck me. I was sitting at my desk, looking at pictures of Maple on my phone instead of working. Her unruly hair stuck up in the back just like Marcus's used to. I realized that I couldn't keep trying to shove their past underneath the proverbial rug. This entire time, I'd been tiptoeing around the facts. I was still trying my damnedest to push all thoughts of Marcus out of this relationship.

But I couldn't keep doing that. Because even though he wasn't walking this earth anymore, he'd never truly be gone. He was in Finley's heart. My memories. A piece of him was in that little girl I loved. It was time to do what was right. I'd been trying to shove him out...when what I needed was to bring him in.

I had a plan.

***

I made it home from work in record time that evening and

found my girls lingering at the kitchen island over their finished plates.

Finley lifted up on her toes and pressed a kiss to my cheek. When she pulled away, the worried look in her eyes almost undid me.

"We've already eaten but I saved you a plate in the oven. It's still warm." She touched my cheek, trying to read the stormy thoughts in my head.

I felt even worse about disappearing on her this morning and leaving her to fend for herself today. "I have somewhere I want to take you guys. Sorry for the short notice, but we've only got a couple hours before it gets dark." And before Maple's bedtime.

"Oh. Okay." Her expression was full of confusion, but she grabbed a handful of damp paper towels and began wiping Maple down. Good, she was going to trust me. "Don't you want to eat something first?"

I shook my head. "Dinner can wait. This is too important. There's something I've got to do if I'm going to be the type of man you both deserve."

A crease formed in her brow as she lifted Maple onto her hip. But she nodded and said, "Okay."

We loaded Maple up in the new car seat I'd gotten for my SUV and headed out of town.

Thirty minutes later, when I slowed and pulled into the cemetery, Finley's eyes widened and she straightened bolt upright in her seat. "Grey?"

I took her hand, lacing her delicate fingers between mine, "You okay?"

She swallowed, her throat bobbing. It was probably as dry as a bone...just like mine. "Yes." She took a deep, heavy breath and then leaned back against the seat again, her eyes darting everywhere as I drove along the little lane leading us to our destination.

I wondered if she'd been here, if she sometimes came to talk to him, or to cry, or to remember the happy times. But I didn't ask. Just because we were in a relationship didn't mean I needed to know every secret she kept. She was entitled to her privacy, especially about sensitive matters like this one.

I parked the car and took a deep breath. "Are you ready?"

She nodded, and without saying anything, went to retrieve Maple from the back. I could only guess what she was thinking.

Everything looked the same – little neat rows of

headstones as far as the eye could see – but I remembered. Our destination lay on the other side of the big maple tree, and we headed straight towards it. I wondered if there was some kind of significance there…. I'd never asked Finley how she chose Maple's name, after all.

It was a beautiful resting place. The leaves offered shade from the scorching summer sun. The wind rustled them, casting dancing spots of light on the grass.

The carved granite headstone glinted in the setting sun.

Finley stopped suddenly several paces behind me and I turned. She lowered Maple to the ground and she took off on unsteady legs, exploring the grassy area beside us. "Come on. It'll be okay," I promised. I took Finley's hand and led her the rest of the way over toward the headstone.

Steeling the nerves I'd been fighting all day, I took a deep breath.

I didn't look at the ground, or the stone marking it, because I knew he wasn't there. Staring out into the distance, I talked to him.

The words came, stilted and self-conscious at first, then more natural as I continued. It was just like old times – me and him, casually sharing what was going on in our lives. Of course, this particular chat was decidedly one-sided. But I knew he wouldn't mind. I held Finley's hand in mine the entire time; I couldn't say who needed that contact more, me or her.

Finally, I reached the moment I'd come here for. The scariest question, the biggest leap of faith.

"Finley has become ... everything to me." I choked up and had to pause for a second. "I'm in love with her, man," I admitted.

A quiet sniff made me look over to see that Finley was crying. Silent tears streaming down her cheeks, making her green eyes shine even brighter.

Maple was chasing a grasshopper nearby, innocently unaware of the heavy moment, so I continued. There was more I needed to say.

My throat tight, I pressed on, "I promise to always protect her and Maple. I promise to be there no matter what. That is my vow. I couldn't save you, but I can save them."

Just then, a songbird flew over and landed on a low branch of the maple tree, not far from where we stood, and gave a quick whistle, catching all of our attention. Plumed in bright blue, that bird whistled a long tune, a sweet high song just for us.

I'd never heard anything like it. Even Maple stopped what she was doing and craned her neck to listen. Then she glanced excitedly between the bird and her mother, her eyes wide with wonder. Her expression seemed to say, *He's trying to tell us something important.*

We both watched it for several minutes, and then Finley's gaze met mine. "It's a sign from Marcus." She smiled, only a little sadly. "He's giving us his blessing."

The most peaceful feeling settled over me and I knew she was absolutely right. I nodded.

"There's something else," I continued. "I want you to know that your little girl will grow up knowing all the best stories from her father. And even though you're not here with us, she'll always have a father's love. She isn't mine, not by blood, but I'll always take care of her."

"Grey ..." Finley's voice broke. "What are you saying?"

"We're going to be a family. I'm going to marry you." I gave her left hand a squeeze, stroking the naked ring finger.

She laughed, her eyes glistening with unshed tears. "Are you sure about that, Mister Archer?"

"I'm positive, Finley Sutton Archer. You two are mine, and I don't want to live any more of my days without you. Now come on, let's go home."

I kissed Finley's temple—she was still staring at me—and then picked up Maple.

The bird continued its magical song the entire walk back to the car.

As if Marcus were really here, as strong as ever, looking down on us. Watching over us. I laced my fingers with Finley's, feeling lighter than I had in a long time. We had our whole lives in front of us—and Marcus wouldn't want us to waste them.

Epilogue

Finley

"Ladies and gentlemen, I present the new Mr. and Mrs. Archer!" the emcee called.

A burst of applause greeted us as Grey led me into the reception tent. The spring sun warmed my shoulders, left bare by my wedding gown, and the breeze played with the curls of my updo. The opening chords of Sinatra's "The Second Time Around" rippled into the open air.

Surrounded by friends and family, we started our first dance. I spotted Nolan and Lacey with Maple among the sea of cheerful faces. It amazed me how much Maple had opened up over the last six months. While she could still be shy at times, she had welcomed "Aunt Lacey" and "Uncle Nolan" into her circle of family. She sat happily on Lacey's lap—what little was left of it. Mrs. Maxwell was due any day now, and she still looked stunning in her pink satin maternity dress. Maple had been fascinated by that bump when she first saw it, gently touching Lacey's belly and staring back at me with huge, questioning eyes. It was a sweet moment.

"You having fun?" Grey murmured as he guided me through a graceful spin.

"Of course," I chuckled.

"So the 'big fuss' was a good idea after all." He gave me a knowing smirk.

I rolled my eyes, though I was still smiling. I had suggested that we just go down to the county courthouse, file our marriage certificate, and be done with it. But Grey had tempted me into a real ceremony with all the trimmings. *I want the world to know*, he'd persuaded. *Just let me spoil you.* And I had to admit, this was awfully nice. I closed my eyes to feel Grey's heartbeat against mine. My husband might be a badass ex-Navy SEAL, but he was also tender and sweet. What a combination.

The song ended all too soon. Our guests clapped again as we took our seats. Maple hopped off Lacey's lap and toddled towards me at warp speed. Somehow her poofy, frilly white dress hadn't gotten dirty yet. I thought she was the cutest flower girl in the history of weddings, but then again, I was pretty biased.

After the buffet was unveiled and everyone had filled their plates, we stood up briefly to thank everyone for coming, then yielded to Nolan for the best man's toast. He stepped in front of the microphone and smoothed his tie.

"I'm going to keep this short and sweet," Nolan said. "My name is Nolan Maxwell, and on behalf of the bride and groom, I'd like to thank you all for coming today. I have the honor of standing with these two fine people as they start their new life together.

"I met both Greyson Archer and Marcus Sutton in my Navy SEAL platoon. Let me say, Finley, that you really know how to pick your men. I've never met two more upstanding soldiers. I trusted them with my life. We've been through hell together...and as many of you know, not all of us made it back.

"But as we honor the fallen, we must never forget to keep on living. Today is a day for celebrating love, happiness, and new beginnings. It was truly the greatest luck that brought you two together. Everyone, please join me in a toast to Mr. and Mrs. Archer: May your marriage be as long as the bride is beautiful." Nolan raised his eyebrows exaggeratedly at Grey. "So I'm afraid you're in this one forever, buddy. Make it count."

Blinking back tears, I laughed and cheered along with the rest of the audience. The emcee waited for the applause to die down before announcing the father-daughter/mother-son dance.

Maple squealed when Grey swept her up. "You ladies enjoy dinner," he said with a wink. "I've got a hot date."

My heart swelled as I watched them on the dance floor. Maple stood on Grey's feet while he held her tiny hands, shuffling back and forth to the music. My bighearted husband, who had once represented the end of my world and now began it anew. My precious daughter, who looked so much like her father sometimes. Past and future together.

"Aren't you going to dance with your dad?" I asked Lacey. Sometimes I felt a little sorry for Nolan, having his boss as a father-in-law. Mr. Barton wasn't an asshole or anything, but he could be pretty intimidating.

Lacey blew a loud sigh. "I would, but..." She patted her round belly with a wry smile. "This one doesn't like exercise. And he's already busy with Brynn. I might take the next song if it's a slow one."

I squinted out at the dance floor. There was Mr. Barton, foxtrotting with the gorgeous girl who had been seated next to Lacey. I couldn't help but giggle; even in the middle of a party, my boss looked so grave. "So that's your sister. I'm glad she could make it."

"Yeah, me too." Lacey sipped her ice water. "Normally she'd be at college or at home, but she decided to visit me for Spring Break."

"Good timing," I commented.

We sat together for a while longer, eating our dinners and watching the dancers, commenting on this or that guest. I was grateful to get off my feet after standing in high heels for the entire ceremony.

When the song ended, the emcee announced that the floor was open to all guests. About half of the dancers headed for the open bar. West, another one of Grey's old SEAL buddies, had graciously offered to provide free drinks and bar service as his wedding gift to us. Grey came back to our table with Maple in tow, plus a whiskey for himself and red wine for me.

I took a sip, but quickly swallowed it to say, "Check that out." I pointed to the bar, where Brynn leaned far over the counter, absorbed in whatever West was saying.

Grey and Lacey both turned their heads.

Lacey chuckled. "Oh, boy. I know that look...Brynn's into him."

Grey studied the scene for a moment, then went back to his whiskey. "It'll never happen."

"Why not?" Lacey asked.

"He just got out of a bad relationship." Grey hesitated. "You didn't hear it from me, but his ex cheated on him. And he's not the type to love easily...it'll take him a while to get over this."

"Oh, that's a damn shame," Lacey sighed.

"I know. Believe me, he needs a good woman in his life."

I nodded in understanding. But I wasn't so sure about Grey's confident proclamation. Even while West served other guests, his eyes rarely left Brynn.

At the squeak of a bakery cart, I put West and Brynn out of my head. The loud buzz of conversation gave way to *oohs* and *ahhs* as the head caterer wheeled the wedding cake into the reception tent. I held my breath as it swayed slightly. The thing was huge. Four tiers of raspberry layer cake with snow-white buttercream frosting, wreathed in green and gold chocolate foliage.

"Attention, everyone," the emcee called, as if the whole party weren't already riveted by the sight. "The bride and groom will now cut their wedding cake."

All eyes fell to us as we walked to the front of the tent, Maple following eagerly behind. The head caterer presented us with the knife and server. Hand in hand, we sank the ornate silver blade into the cake's bottom tier. Then Grey plated the slice and raised a fluffy bite to my lips.

Staring deep into his adoring eyes, I savored this first sweet taste of the rest of our lives.

About the Author

A *New York Times*, *Wall Street Journal*, and *USA TODAY* best-selling author of more than twenty titles, Kendall Ryan has sold more than a million e-books, and her books have been translated into several languages in countries around the world. She's a traditionally published author with Simon & Schuster and Harper Collins UK, as well as an independently published author.

Since she first began self-publishing in 2012, she's appeared at #1 on Barnes & Noble and iBooks charts around the world. Her books have also appeared on the *New York Times* and *USA TODAY* best-seller list more than two dozen times. Ryan has been featured in such publications as *USA TODAY*, *Newsweek*, and *In Touch Weekly*.

Stay Connected

Website: www.kendallryanbooks.com

Facebook: Kendall Ryan Books

Twitter: @kendallryan1

Other Books by Kendall Ryan

WHEN I BREAK Series:

When I Break

When I Surrender

When We Fall

FILTHY BEAUTIFUL LIES Series:

Filthy Beautiful Lies

Filthy Beautiful Love

Filthy Beautiful Lust

Filthy Beautiful Forever

LESSONS WITH THE DOM Series:

The Gentleman Mentor

Sinfully Mine

STAND-ALONE NOVELS:

Hard to Love

Reckless Love

Resisting Her

The Impact of You

Screwed

Monster Prick

CPSIA information can be obtained at www.ICGtesting.com
Printed in the USA
BVOW06s1235200616

452634BV00028BA/307/P